AEDAN

HARRISON AMBUSH BOOK 3

KATHI S. BARTON

World Castle Publishing, LLC
Pensacola, Florida
Copyright © Kathi S. Barton 2016
Hardback ISBN: 9781629895055
Paperback ISBN: 9781629895062
eBook ISBN: 9781629895079
First Edition World Castle Publishing, LLC, June 25, 2016
http://www.worldcastlepublishing.com
Licensing Notes
Cover: Karen Fuller
Editor: Maxine Bringenberg

CHAPTER 1

Aedan smiled when he saw all the flyers that had his name on them being put into yards. *Aedan Harrison for Governor*. Who would have thought that only a short three weeks ago he'd been working for his brother's firm, and now he was not just running for governor, but he was also having a grand time of it. He saw his dad coming out of his political offices and had to smile when he showed him the new signage.

"I had to give them a little grief 'bout the picture. You look like a little boy in them, and I thought about having them paint a mustache on you or something; but your mom, she liked them so we went with it." He nodded at his dad, proud as he could be about what was going on, but also a little overwhelmed. "All you boys really take good pictures. It's in your blood. I think it's a trait that I passed down to you, what do you think?"

Four days ago there had been an ad on television about Aedan running in the upcoming election. He was getting a late start, he knew that, but he was getting a lot of support too. The president had been in the commercial, saying that Aedan was a man of men and that he would do the best job possible for the state. Aedan had sat there for nearly an hour after it had aired just thinking about how fast this was all going down. Then he'd gotten up, done a little dance, and gone to run with his brother, Darcy, who had been staying with him for a few weeks. He didn't mention anything about seeing the ad until they were having beers and pizza at his house later. Then after polishing off two large with every kind of meat on them, they'd talked.

"You think that when the time comes, you'll be sitting in the big house?" Aedan said nothing. Not that he hadn't been having the same thoughts, but he was terrified to say the words out loud. Even to his brothers. Darcy laughed as he continued, "You have a sappy look on your face. The same one you get when you've figured out what you're getting for Christmas from Mom and Dad. Just so you know, you're going to have to be better at the poker look if you're having thoughts that big."

"I just want to get this election under my belt, then I can go from there." Darcy only nodded, but he did have a smile that said a lot. "How are things going with you and the new building? I'm thinking that in no time you're going to have your own mailbox out front. Not that I'm in any hurry for you to leave here. I love hanging out with you."

"Storm is having it made up as we speak, believe it or not. She said to consider it a building warming gift. Did I tell you that she's going to help me with finding furniture for the building? I asked for things that would blend well with the old building, and she had this amazing desk delivered yesterday. I'm going to love being in my own place but still working for the family. Christ, she really does know people who know

people."

They both laughed, and Darcy asked about his first duty in office when he won.

"I'm thinking we need more jobs, don't you? But as for Storm, she really does know just about everyone. And she's being very pushy about things beyond the governorship. I'm not thinking along those lines yet. I have done some research on my opponent. He's not very...well, I was going to say very trustworthy, but I think he's underhanded and a jackass as well." Darcy said nothing. "You know him?"

"I do, sort of. And this is between the two of us, but if you want to find some true dirt about him, you should look into the people who used to work for him. Both professionally as well as at his home. I understand that they're the same, they both work for him, but I'm talking about his different staffers." Aedan wasn't sure that he wanted to sling mud, and Darcy handed him a file. "I got this in my inbox at work today. It's a questionnaire. I'm pretty sure that as your brother I wasn't meant to get it, but there are some pretty in-depth questions there."

He told his brother that he'd look into the people but didn't pick up the file just yet. He wasn't even sure that he wanted to. Darcy took the decision out of his hands after it sat there for several more minutes and picked up the paperwork and flipped through it to the back. Aedan wasn't sure what he was doing until he handed it to him. Aedan read the first three questions, then looked at Darcy.

"They asked you what you thought my sexual preferences were?" Darcy nodded. "What the hell does that have to do with anything? I mean, how the hell does he get by with asking those sort of personal questions?"

"Don't know, but there are a lot more in there. Read on.

7

At one point they ask me if I thought you were going to have affairs while in the seat. I'm thinking that if they get one person to answer yes to that, you're going to be labeled as a pervert as well as some sort of sexual deviant. Whoever sent this out is fishing, and they don't care what sort of catch they get. I'm having someone look into it." Aedan laughed. "No, not Storm. If she gets wind of this there will be hell to pay."

"Yeah, she's a little overprotective when it comes to us. But this shit, it's not the way I want to do things, Darcy. You know me. I'd never want to stoop this low." He read a few more questions until he got to the last one. "It asks if there are any things that the reader can think of that might be helpful to the people of this town. There's a number here they can call."

"Yep. And I called." Darcy leaned back in the couch that had only been delivered that morning. "They're asking more questions too. Like how long have you been a drug addict. They're not asking *if* you were, but how long you've been using. And when was the last time I'd shot up with you, and where that might have been. I assured the person that I'd never even seen you take an aspirin and they laughed. This guy told me that he had enough people calling in to talk to them that they knew that wasn't true. Whoever is working to smear you, they're not playing very fairly. Like I said, any of this gets out, lies or not, it's not going to go well for you or the family. Storm will be the least of their problems when Mom and Dad find out."

"No shit." He leaned back as well. "I wonder who it is. I mean, with this kind of work, someone is really out to make me look bad. I'm sure if I asked Ellison he'd say something like 'well, I don't know' in his best *you're a moron* voice. Any ideas who I might have to have murdered?"

"Nope. As I said, I'm having someone look. Mason, too,

is having a little fun with this. He said to tell you when it hits his inbox, he's going to answer all the questions in his own language and hopes someone there gets a kick out of it. He's been in and out of the offices for a couple of days now; I've not really found out why, but it's fun having him around. Mason said that he's helping out while Riordan is out of town." Aedan asked when he'd be back. "Don't know. Storm has been out of the country for a few days too. But I think she's coming back tomorrow. The president has them doing something overseas, and I think they're going to make a little vacation of it too."

He'd spoken to Darcy, and now it was two days past when they were to have returned home and neither Storm nor Riordan was back yet. Something had come up, they'd been told. He'd never found out what it was, but he knew that it was like them to rest up after they were done working. Even Dad had been saying how he wished he'd had such perks. Then he and Mom had gone to wherever it was to help out.

Aedan was getting things put away in the kitchen when he heard someone in the drive. The house had a very long drive, lined with trees and a big fucking gate at the end, so he knew that whoever was here had made an effort in coming to see him. Going out to the back deck that wrapped around the entire house, he watched. While the car was in front of the garage, he stood there while whoever it was decided to either get out or drive away. The elderly man that finally got out of the car was no one he knew.

He stood with the car door opened and his hands on the door. Both of them. He looked more like he was hanging on rather than just taking in the view. Aedan decided that tomorrow he was going to have someone manning the gate house as Storm had told him to do weeks ago.

"Can I help you?" The man looked around like he was

trying to decide if they were alone or not. Just as he was ready to ask again, another car pulled in the drive and he was relieved to see it was Darcy. Neither man spoke, but his brother did come up on the deck with him. "Perhaps you're at the wrong address."

"No, I'm where I'm to be. I'm here to meet someone else. It's important that nobody knows where I am, you see, and I was told that I'd be okay here for a little while." Aedan nodded. "You're the boy, the one running for governor. I saw the signs in people's yards. Congratulations on that. But you need to get yourself someone to man that gate down there. Doesn't do you squat if anyone can come in here uninvited."

"I was just thinking the same thing when you pulled up. Who are you?" The man looked worn out. Depressed too, like he wanted to curl into a ball and simply give up. Aedan had no idea where those thoughts had come from, but he had a feeling that they were all true. Making his way off the deck, Darcy was with him but he stayed back, like he was going to be ready should anything happen. When Aedan was nearly to the man he smelled it…blood. Old and fresh. "Are you hurt?"

"Yes. I got shot a couple of days ago. I thought for sure that I was a goner, but I managed to get myself free. I've been on the run since, not able to stop the hole in me other than to press a towel or two on it. Hurts like someone has been doing a jig on my insides. You're not human." Aedan shook his head and looked the man over. "I can manage to move in a bit, but I have to rest up if you're planning to kick me to the curb."

"All right, I won't kick you anywhere so long as you don't give me a reason to. Besides, I don't think you'd make it if I did. I can help you, if you'd allow it." He just shook his head and continued to hold onto the door that he was near. "Who are you meeting? Maybe I can call them for you."

"It's me, Aedan." He looked at Mason as he made his way to the elderly man. "He's a stubborn old coot, but I owe someone to keep him safe. Otherwise I would have left his sorry ass on the side of the road." The older man laughed and then coughed hard enough to make Aedan think he was in a great deal more pain than he was letting on.

Aedan had no idea why he thought that Mason was lying about his feelings toward the stranger. But Mason picked him up in his arms and asked Aedan if he could use his house. Before he could figure out why the man was here or who he was, Mason had taken him to one of the spare bedrooms on the second floor and laid the now unconscious man on the bed.

"I'll call Ennis."

Darcy left the room when it was apparent that the man was really hurt. Mason pulled up his shirt and they both looked at the wounds. He had indeed been shot; twice, as a matter of fact. And both wounds were seeping enough to make Aedan realize that he might have used more than a couple of towels to try and stop the bleeding.

"His name is Neal. Paddy Neal. He's an old friend of a friend that…Browning asked me to bring him here as they're not home yet. I would have taken him to my place, but it's too out in the open as yet. He needs a place to hide out until I can get him somewhere safe." Aedan asked him why here. "Because, my dear friend, your house is built like a fortress and I have been here before, so had you not been home, I could have entered and put him up. It really is important that he is safe."

"I don't understand why he isn't in a hospital, or at the very least a clinic somewhere." Mason wasn't one to explain himself, and this time was no different. As they both waited on Ennis to arrive with his black bag, they stripped Paddy's clothing off. Mason told Aedan what he knew…or in this case, what he wanted Aedan to know.

"Just over a week ago there was a shooting. Nothing you would have heard about here, but an undercover cop was shot several times in the chest at close range. She was about the best there was, but the bad guys didn't care for her. This is her grandda. Paddy was on the phone with her when she was taken out and presumed killed. She wasn't, but not for lack of them trying. Just as they were ready to put one in her head, I arrived and took her away to someplace else." Aedan felt like he was in one of those carnival rides that spun you about so quickly you couldn't figure out up or down. "She's critical, in grave condition actually, but she is going to pull through. But as far as the world is concerned, the world that she works in, she's dead. And we need to keep it that way for a little while longer. I also have her phone."

"Her phone." Mason nodded as he sat down on the other chair in the room. Aedan had already taken the other. "And this is making sense to me how? In the event you didn't notice, this is not a hospital. I have no staff here that can help out, and I'm pretty sure that since you said you'd been here before, you know that this house isn't equipped to have guests just yet. The only reason I have this room is because I got a great deal on this set at an auction."

"This house is very old, and at one time, many decades even before your father was a glint in anyone's eye, this house was owned by a very dear and close friend of mine. We had many…well, let's just say that if these walls could talk, you'd be out of here in a minute." This wasn't funny and Aedan said that to him. "No, it's not. But as I was saying, when Nikki was shot and presumably killed, they went after her grandda when her body and the phone that she used came up missing. I took her someplace safe, as I said, to make sure she would get the care that she needed. Also, I have taken care that the phone isn't found. She has some pretty determined enemies because of what she's found out about one of the drug dealers in her city. And trust me when I tell you, his little Nikki is one hell of an investigator."

"Okay, let me get this straight. This undercover agent was murdered but not. Her grandda was shot to hell and you brought him here. And now, for whatever reason, you think he needs to stay here while he either recuperates or dies, and I'm supposed to keep quiet about it." Mason grinned and nodded. "You do know that I'm running for governor, right? And this is just the kind of shit that my opponent is looking for to bury me in, correct?"

"You will be fine, young Aedan. And I'd not worry about the questionnaires either. I've taken care that none of those questions ever get out in public." Aedan asked Mason how he knew that. "Let's just say that I know more people than Browning does, and mine are a bit more ruthless than she is. And as for Paddy being here, it's because the president and Browning asked me to bring him here for you to keep safe. They have a great deal more confidence in you than you appear to have in yourself."

That wasn't quite true, but Aedan was nervous about having a bleeding stranger in his house. He knew that his family would cover for him in the event someone found out. And if the shit hit the fan, like Mason was suggesting, then they'd be there for him as well.

When Ennis came in a few minutes later, Darcy asked to speak to Aedan. As soon as they entered the hallway, leaving Mason and his other brother to deal with Paddy, Darcy started pacing the long hall. Darcy was a thinker, one who did not blurt out whatever was on his mind until he was sure of his facts.

"I think this is my fault." Aedan asked him how when Mason had told the man to come here. "I helped him. In a way. You know how I love the news? And especially ones that have to do with syndicates and shit like that? Well, Mason knew as well."

"Go on." His brother really did have a fixation on things in the news. He had an app on his computer both here and at home that would tell him every major thing going down. Even his phone and car were rigged up with it. "If you tell me that you called Mason when this went down, I'm going to brain you."

"I didn't. Mason called me about a week ago. He said that he had an idea that something was going to go down with a friend that was working undercover. And that he wanted me to keep an ear out for something, anything, that might have to do with this certain city…Chicago. So when the call came in that an officer was down, I contacted him right away and told him what I knew. I think he went to get him or something." He told him it was apparently a woman. "Okay, that makes sense. He probably had some affair with her and now he's protecting her or something. Whatever it is, I think this man had something to do with it. Because a couple of hours later, I hear the name again, this time they say it's at a residence and shots are being fired. I let Mason know and now the man shows up here. What do you suppose this is about?"

"I don't know. He just told me that the president and Storm told him to bring the undercover person's grandda here." Darcy just nodded, but looked as confused as Aedan felt. "I'm guessing they have something to do with him then.

All I know is that I have a wounded man in my house that I know nothing about, as well as some woman out there that may or may not be dead. And I'm to keep quiet about it so that they'll be safe. I have no problem with that, but I wish I had more information."

The door opened behind them and Mason stood there. He looked injured, and that was when Aedan realized it was daylight and he was out in the sunlight. When he leaned back against the wall, seemingly exhausted, he and Darcy helped him to the lower levels and away from most of the sunlight. He took a seat but refused their offer of blood.

"She is not my lover, though once I had a look at the little morsel, I had thoughts of changing her and taking her to my bed. But alas, I cannot. She is off limits to me." Aedan asked why. "She is the niece and goddaughter of the president. The man presently in your bedroom is his father. They're keeping their identities quiet because of what they do and did for a living."

Aedan nodded then shook his head. The niece and dad of the president? What else would he find out, that they were also aliens from another planet? Shaking his head to try and clear some of it up only made it worse. He was beginning to have a headache right between his eyes. And he never got headaches.

"Why here? Why not in some other house, closer to him? Or for that matter, why not in a hospital? And what do you mean, did and do? This is like being on a loop de loop ride and you can't get off; you know that, don't you?" Mason said nothing but leaned back on the couch. Aedan started to demand answers, but he sat down too and thought about things. "It's because of this woman being undercover, isn't it? Something about that is why they have to be protected.

She knows something or has.... The phone...you mentioned the phone. You're thinking that whatever is on it might be something someone would need to bring them in. And those people, the ones on the phone, need to think them dead. For now, like you said, they need to be safe to heal and to be able to bring this to light later. And if the people after them knew differently, then shit would hit the fan."

"I would say that you're onto it, at least I think. As I said before, I don't know a great many of the details. Other than I was asked by Browning to keep an eye out for her. It was most difficult since this cop mostly worked during the daylight hours. But I knew that young Darcy here had an ear for this, so I asked him to have a listen for me." Aedan looked at his brother then back at Mason. "I only had to give him a name and the city. The rest, it was up to him. He might well have saved her life by being diligent in this. And most assuredly her grandfather. I'm sorry to say that I was too weak to bring him to you quickly. Taking Nikki away the way that I did drained me badly. Driving here was the only way he could have made it. Thankfully he had taken precautions, and had another car with money and clothing it in for them both."

"And this man, he is involved how? I mean, other than being her grandfather, how is it he has been shot? Being in the wrong place at the wrong time?" Mason said he only knew a few details. "Do I need to know them? Or better yet, do I want to know them?"

"I would say not." Mason stood up. "There will be staff coming here to care for him and your household. Not from me, but from the president. He doesn't want you to have to worry about things, so he has asked a butler to come in and take care of things here should you want. He said to call it a thank you gift. I know Basford; he and his wife are good

people."

"All right, but to be honest, I'm not sure what I need at this point. I've only been here for a few months. I mean, Howard is a good friend of the family, but I don't really need someone to take over my house." Mason said he figured he'd say that. "How do I give him updates on his dad?"

"That won't be necessary at this point. He said that he will contact you when the time is right. But for now, it is safer for his dad to not be associated with him. Not because he's done anything wrong, nothing like that, but he should like to keep him safe. And he knows he will be here." Aedan had a thought, not a good one. Mason laughed. "You have many things running through that head of yours, my friend. I would suggest that you not read anything into this other than a good friend needed your help. You know as well as I that Howard is a good man. If he had not been, Browning would have ended him long ago."

Aedan was still sitting on his couch when someone came into the room with him. He only stared at the man, not having any idea if he should have been frightened, taken cover, or put out his hand in friendship. His head was going in so many directions he wasn't sure which way was up.

"My name is Basford, my lord. You were told that I was coming?" He nodded. "Mason sent us to help out around the house. Cook and clean for you should you need it, and hire a staff should you want that as well. I'm to understand from him that you have a large household and may need more than just me in residence."

"To be honest with you Basford, I have no idea what I need." The man only nodded. "Do you know what's going on here, with the man upstairs then?"

"I do. I have been informed that should he need something

17

more than he has at the moment, I'm to make a few calls." More than Aedan knew, and he said as much. "Mason said that you were slightly overwhelmed and that you may need a little guidance until you are settled."

"That might not ever happen." Basford nodded. "I'd really like to have some breakfast, then while I'm eating, perhaps you and I can figure out what I do with a butler and cook. While I know the duties of both, I'm not sure how to go about getting things done. Does that make sense?"

"It does. I have met the new cook at your parents' house, as well as their butler there. Mr. Shaw has been a good friend of mine for many years." That was helpful. Shaw had been working for his family for decades. "Shall we go to the kitchen and see where we stand there? My wife, she's here as well and has asked to do a bit of cooking for you. She's not up to the standards of the young new Mrs. Harrison, but she said she can fill your belly."

He was talking about Andi, Mac's wife. Nodding once, he got up to follow the man. Whatever was going on right now, he thought it best if he just played along. For now, anyway.

As they entered the kitchen, he thought again about why the president would have sent the man here. Aedan wondered if he thought that just because he had endorsed him for the governorship that he could take advantage of him. Not that it was a huge hardship having Paddy in his home, but it was odd that the man had been shot and needed to hide out. Then there was the undercover cop thing too. Why was she presumed to be dead? And who wanted her that way? As he sat down to wait for his breakfast, a notebook and pen was set before him. He looked up at the woman, who also handed him a large glass of orange juice.

"To make notes with. Winnie said that you were going

18

to figure things out." He asked her who Winnie was. "My husband. His name is Winfred, but I call him Winnie. My name is Rose, Rose Basford. Would you like for me to call him Basford as well?"

"No. I like Winnie too. It sounds less…I don't know. Less stiff. I'm new to this having a staff thing." She smiled at him and he felt comforted by it. "My parents, you know them as well?"

"Oh yes. Well, not personally, but I know of them. It's Browning that we know better. Her family would hire us when the staff was in flux. Happened a great deal at the beginning of their tenure in the mansion. But Winnie and I were never up to snuff for them. Only good enough…I should not be speaking of her parents so poorly. Forgive me." He told her it was fine. He'd heard they were a little cold. "Browning— it was what we called her for so long after they passed—she wasn't what they wanted in a child. Daring and full of spit and vinegar. Once, when she was about four, we'd been there for a couple of days when she came into the house with not just a snake in her hand, but a turtle as well. Told us right off if we dared cook them for her supper, she'd have us put before a firing squad. I have never laughed so hard in my life."

When Winnie cleared his throat, his wife moved to the stove. But before pulling out things from the fridge, she kissed Winnie on the cheek and made him blush. Aedan thought he'd enjoy having them around as much as he did his parents.

It took them two hours to get things squared away. And when Ennis came to join them, he was fed as well. Darcy had gone to work, saying that he'd be back late because he had to find a place to live, and had his eye on a building or two in the downtown area. He'd been saying that for nearly the three weeks that he'd been sleeping over here.

"Your guest is resting right now. I took out the bullets and gave them to Mason when he came back for them. He said he'd take care that they got into the right hands. Mr. Neal is going to be down for a few more days, so I've made arrangements to have a nurse brought in. Also through Mason. He'll just need help getting up and down and his dressing changed. I'll come see him a couple of times a day if you don't mind. Just to make sure he's healing all right."

"You don't want to do this." Ennis said that he really didn't mind. That he owed Mason. "Everyone seems to owe him. How is it he's indebted to you?"

"The new building that I'm moving into? It has a lair in the sublevels. I mean, really, it's an apartment with all the things that you'd find anywhere, except no windows. I've given him permission to live there for as long as I own the building. It's safer for him, he said, than the aunts' house." Lynn and Sally, aunts of Stormy, had been letting Mason stay in their basement while he was in the area. And he'd been having repairs done on the house in return. "He said that he'd take care of the taxes for me, but I said I just felt better with him living there. Sort of a safety net should I need it in the event the place is robbed. I'll have a lot of drugs in the place when I'm done moving in. Oh yeah, that reminds me, I have to talk to an attorney about something. I got this letter in the mail about something to do with drugs on the premises. Did you ever hear of a vault for drugs in a business like mine? Huge sucker, too, if I'm reading this right."

"No. I mean, I guess that makes sense, but it's not like you're going to be selling them, right? We're talking just things like samples and such." Ennis said that was it, but he had to get one. "I'd check into it like you are. Probably just a precautionary letter they send to all doctors."

20

After his brother left, Aedan went to check up on his new guest and wasn't surprised to find him resting comfortably. Getting ready to go into the office himself, Aedan thought about all the things that could go wrong with this. First and foremost, he could be out of the running for a job that he'd come to want very badly.

CHAPTER 2

Otis looked around the war room that he'd had set up to find the fucking cop. Maps, notes, and anything else that they could think of were marked on large sheets of paper that had been brought in. Places where they had thought she might be but wasn't were marked, as well as other places to check. So far, nothing. He wasn't sure where else they could look. Otis thought for sure she was dead — they'd certainly fired enough bullets into her body — but what they should have done was put one between her eyes and been done with it. Whatever had happened to her body while she laid there was anyone's guess. She had simply disappeared.

"We've been by her grandfather's place several times since we went by to talk to him, and nothing. No one in any hospital has seen him, no animal doctors, not even any would be doctors have had any suspicious men in to be worked on. I know that he can't be up and around for long. He took at least two shots from my gun for sure. It's like the girl. Just gone." Otis nodded, but said nothing to his man, Joe. "I have a theory, if you want to hear it."

"I do, but in a minute. Let me tell you what I think, and then we can add to it with your theory. I'm thinking that they're not together. Whoever took them, and I'm thinking it's just one person, he would have had to separate them so that we'd not have them where we want them. I've also been thinking that perhaps she might not be dead. You said yourself that there wasn't enough blood left behind for her to be over the fucking rainbow. So, like the grandfather, she's getting medical care somewhere. But where?"

"She had to have a vest on. It's the only thing that fits." That was what Otis thought now too. Christ, the woman acted like everyone was out to get her. "Oh, and we can't find her phone. I'm pretty sure you were right in saying that she was flashing pictures of all of us. That alone will get us all in deep shit. I'm almost afraid to think who might have that now."

"You've not said anything to anyone about that, have you?" He said that he hadn't and wouldn't. "Good. What is it you think happened to her? And the other Neal?"

"Vamp." Otis turned and looked at him. His fear of those monsters was known to everyone who ever heard his name. Otis Adkins was terrified of vampires. Any shifters really, but it was the vamps and their long sharp teeth that had his bladder tightening up. "Yeah, I know what you're thinking. Just why not kill us all while he was there? But he had to get this woman to some doc somewhere. Right? He might have even given her a little of himself to keep her alive until the phone appears. After that comes to light, then he can do what he wants to her. But I'm thinking…well, if he saved her, then maybe she's something to him."

"What would he want with an undercover cop?" Joe said he had no idea, but how else would she have simply disappeared while they were standing over her. "I don't know. And to be honest, I fucking don't care what he wanted with her. But I can't have her out there. Not alive, anyway. And the fact that we were too slow to realize about the camera does not set well with me, as you can well imagine. We were told that when undercover cells were left at the station. What the fuck is the one that we got from her desk there, a burner?"

"I would imagine. I've been having one of your computer guys looking into the lost phone a little more. They said that she was on the line with someone, her grandfather as it turns out, when we started on her, but it doesn't appear that anyone has used it since. And no matter what he does, he can't find it. Pinging it or something like that. Either it's been destroyed, which we can only hope for, or someone with more smarts than we got here has it deep in some hole."

He doubted that anyone was smarter than the men he employed. And if they were, he'd find them and bring them in to work for him, or kill them. Either way, he had the best of the best. If they had no idea where the phone was, he was going to assume that it was destroyed. It might let him sleep at night knowing that one thing was going his way.

After Joe left him to find out what he could about the grandfather, Otis went into the living room and sat on his couch to think. Almost as soon as he was seated a drink was brought to him and the fireplace was turned on. Christ, he loved having all the comforts of money. But it would soon be gone if he didn't find that girl. Even now he was having some income issues that he could not figure out.

It had been five days since he'd been informed that Nikki was going to be out of reach to anyone that would help her, and two since the shoot-out. One way or the other Neal had been a pain in his ass for nearly two decades. And just when he had her where he'd been wanting her, she disappeared without a trace. And so had the only other person that would know where she was.

Paddy Neal had been about the best cop he'd had the displeasure of hiding from. Fat lot of good it had done him. Just a year after Paddy had joined the force, he'd made a name for himself by rooting out all the bad cops in the big house. Ten of Otis's best men, all working for him, had been sent to prison. Sent, but never to be heard from again, thankfully.

It had taken him nearly five years to find himself another crew and have enough on them that they knew better than to turn him in, and now another fucking Neal comes in and does the same shit. Lucky for Otis the captain knew how to play ball, or he wouldn't have even known about the bitch.

It had cost Otis a great many favors being called in to have each and every one of the first group of cops killed. Less for the second, but he hated to spend money needlessly. He kept waiting for someone to connect the dots, ones that would tell someone that he'd been paying people to kill the rogue cops, but had found out just recently that the state didn't really care how they died so long as they were gone from their books. He'd done them a favor, he supposed, one that he'd never be able to collect on.

Then the fucking granddaughter had come along, and not only had she gotten him caught with his pants down, so to speak, but with the smoking gun with this latest shit. And if he didn't find her before someone else did, or figured out about the phone, he was going back to prison, and it was doubtful that he'd ever come out unless it was in a long black bag with a one-way zipper.

His informant—her boss—had told Otis that she was close to having all her ducks in a row to bring him in. So close that she had two of his tweeters, men that only answered to him, asking to be taken out of the station so that they wouldn't be caught. These were men, when he needed them to be, hitmen and drug dealers as well. Both tweeters were now dead, of course. Otis never left behind evidence, and he hated men who jumped ship before he said they could. And now he had to deal with the fact that the bitch had taken his picture. And all because she'd taken James Street and not Upland like he'd thought she would.

They'd been headed there when his driver had spotted her coming out of the little shop with a loaf of bread under her arm, of all things. He wondered now what might have happened if they had waited on her. Gotten her on her own street, right in front of her house. It was a moot point now, but it was something that stuck in his craw.

Then the bitch had pissed him off more because she'd not sounded like she was afraid. Of him or dying. When she'd offered to take him in if he turned himself over to her, he'd felt his temper, never the best anyway, snap. He had shot her first. And that was going to be his biggest downfall if he didn't find the bitch. He was pretty sure that hitting her in the leg had left behind something that would come back to bite him in the ass.

Otis was one of the big-time drug dealers in the city. He wasn't as untouchable as a couple of others in the area, but he was quickly making a name for himself by taking over the smaller territories that they didn't bother with and expanding his working area. And when he'd told the bigger dealers and suppliers that he was going to have Nikki where he wanted her, they'd joined him on the street that morning. Christ, that had been his first of many mistakes concerning the cop.

When he'd been told her regular route — go to the store, buy dinner, then home — he'd been ready to take her as soon as she was on her own quiet street that had been devoid of everyone that had been home. She was as regular as his daily shit. When she finished with a case, she would do the same fucking thing. It would have been perfect but for the fact that she'd gone the wrong fucking way. Lucky, or maybe unluckily for him, they were headed there when she turned up in front of them.

They were ill prepared for her, and had gone off the cuff and shot her with witnesses galore to see them do it. Not that it stopped them from doing what they'd gone there to do, kill the fucking bitch. There had been enough big names with him to have people turning their backs on what was going down, he knew that. No one, as far as he knew, had ever come forward with any information on who the men were, who had been holding the guns, or where the hell the woman was that had supposedly bled all over the street. He supposed it paid to have enough gun power that when you told people not to say a word or else, they knew you meant it. And now she was gone.

He supposed if a vampire had come to get her, and snatched her away, then that would explain a great deal. No one, no matter how many times he'd wished it, just simply disappeared without a single trace. Not even when you buried them in concrete in new construction sites. Nor when you dropped them over the side of your boat when you were out for the day with the family. Everything found a way to pop up at the worse possible times.

Speed; it would have taken a great deal of it to get her and get out without anyone seeing anything. The fact that the vamp, if there was one, had gotten her during the daylight hours and wasn't ash said he was old. And age meant magic. Otis was dealing with a vampire that not only was involved, but a very powerful one as well. Fuck, this was all he needed. Another person after his ass.

His wife, Savannah, and daughter, Dorothea, came into the living room when he was just ready to go to his office. He felt like a deer in the headlights when they saw him. Usually he never ventured far from his office; it was where he hid out when they were in the house. Otis loved them with all his heart, but with the impending wedding, he wanted to strangle them on a daily basis.

"We're having a problem. And I need for you to fix it." He told his wife that he'd try. "No, Otis, I need it fixed, not for you to try. This is our baby girl's big day, and it's going to be ruined if you don't fix it. And I think you're the only one that can."

He looked at his daughter, Dorothea, the pride and joy of his life. And to be honest, he could not wait for someone else to take over her maintenance for a change. He was glad that Robert Trevino had a nice pot of money at his disposal, because she was expensive. And with the troubles that he'd been having of late with the police that were not on his payroll, it was becoming imperative that he do something to cut some of his outgoing money. His wife and daughter could go through a million dollars without blinking an eye, and it had to stop. He had no idea what to do about it either, short of taking away their credit cards, and that wasn't going to happen unless it was a last straw.

"What is the problem, pumpkin? Daddy will do his best to make it right." She sobbed, just as he expected her to whenever things weren't going her way. Otis looked as his wife and saw something that startled him. Hatred. But it was there and gone so quickly that he was sure he'd been mistaken. "What's happened?"

"Well, the cake that we ordered over six months ago might not be ready when we need it." If memory served him right, the wedding was still about three or four months away. Valentine's Day if he was correct. "They said that the flowers she wanted for the bottom tier might not be in bloom then, and they want to substitute another one for it. The same color he said, but not the right flower. That's not the way we do things; substitution is not an option when it comes to our little girl's wedding day, Otis. You need to make sure that it's right. Pay him, or give me cash and I'll pay him to get it right."

Otis looked at his wife then at his daughter, who was now sobbing in earnest. A flower was causing this much commotion? Did they not realize that his life was on the line and there might not be a fucking wedding? But instead of telling them this, he let out a long breath and thought about what he was going to say.

"Daddy, you have to make it so the flowers that I want are there. I want you to make him get them." He wasn't even sure what he'd do, but said nothing. "This will be a disaster and will ruin everything for me. We'll have to start from the beginning if you can't make this right for me. I'll need a new dress. The bridesmaids will have to have new dresses to match mine. The invitations won't go with everything else. Those flowers were important to me."

He had already shelled out over fifty grand on the dresses alone. There wasn't any way he was going to have them start over. It was not that he couldn't afford this…at least right now he could. But if the raids on his shipments and his drugs going into storage at the station house and not out on the street for him to cash in on continued, he was going to be fucked.

Christ, he shuddered when he thought of the countless taste testings that he'd had to go to. There would be no getting out of it this time either. Who the fuck really cared if the cake was chocolate with raspberries or strawberries? Just say the *I do's* and be done with the whole damned thing.

"Now, I'm not trying to cause any uproar here, but what do these flowers have that the ones he can use don't? Don't be mad at me, I'm only asking so I know what we're working with here." His wife pulled out her phone and showed him the two pictures she had of the flowers that were picked out and the ones the baker needed to use. He swapped them back and forth three times, trying his best to find something, anything, that looked different. Hell, even the backgrounds behind them looked exactly alike. He looked at his little girl. "Honey, I don't see any difference."

"Oh, Daddy. You just have to. Mom saw it right away." He studied them hard now, enlarging them so that he could see one thing that wasn't alike. Nothing. "You just don't understand how important this is to me. They're as different as night and day."

Not to him. But instead of saying that he wasn't seeing it, he told them both that he'd work to make it right. He'd bet his next shipment coming in that if he were to tell the baker to use the new flower, no one would know the difference. Feeling pretty good about his solution to the problem, he escaped to his office. He might even have a cot brought in to stay there until this wedding was over.

~~~

Paddy looked around the room he was in. Not moving until he was sure of what had been going on since he'd gotten here, wherever here was, he thought about his granddaughter. She'd been killed. His heart broke for her and he felt tears fall down his face.

"Mr. Neal?" He turned his head slowly to the right to look

at the man he'd not noticed being there. "My name is Aedan Harrison. You're in my home."

"Is there anyone here looking for me?" He shook his head and stood up, stretching as he did. "Christ, you're a big man. Ever have anyone tell you that?"

"My mother. You should see my older brother, Riordan. He's about three inches taller." Paddy started to sit up, feeling at a disadvantage laying down with this man towering over him. "You're to be as still as you can. If you want up I can help you, but you shouldn't try to move too much on your own. My brother, Ennis—he's a doctor—he said he'd knock me on my ass if he had to come back here again and put in new stitches."

"I got up before." Aedan nodded. "I remember that now. Had to piss like.... I do now, too, as a matter of fact. Think you can help an old man out?"

He laughed. "Old man? I think not. Ennis said you're fit for a man about half your age. And that he's never heard of a person driving across the state bleeding as bad as you were and still being as feisty. His words, not mine. Let me get you up and going. But let's go easily this time. I don't want to have the shit knocked out of me if my brother comes back."

Aedan helped him to the bathroom, and when he shut the door behind him, Aedan said he'd be right outside the door if he needed him. He'd been all right moving along the floor, weak but moving. But standing here now with his dick in his hand and his body as weak as a kitten, Paddy was pretty sure that he might have to drag his ass back to the bed before he was done. And more than likely, the kid would have to carry him too.

Finishing up, he turned on the water after flushing and held onto the sink. With a quick knock to the door, Aedan came in but didn't touch him. Paddy was glad for the man being kind enough not to point out how shitty he looked. Paddy looked in the mirror again before standing up as straight as he could and hobbling back to the bedroom on his own. The only way to get stronger was to get over the weakness, he used to tell his— He stopped that thought.

"Mind if I sit for a spell? I mean, I know that I should be lying down and all, but I want to talk if you'll let me. Don't even care if it's about the weather for now, just need to hear a voice." Aedan led him to the chair that he'd been sitting in and helped him sit. When Aedan got the small coverlet from the bottom of the bed, Paddy allowed him to cover his legs up, being that they were bare assed naked. Paddy, not one to hang out in only his boxers, was grateful to be covered up.

"My cook is bringing you up something to eat. I'm afraid that it won't be much right now. Ennis said you can have some broth and some tea if you want. Just liquid until you heal a bit more." He asked how long he'd been here. "This is the third morning. The first time you woke up, yesterday, Ennis had been here having dinner with me and Darcy, my other brother. He gave you something to knock you out again and told me to keep an eye on you. We don't have your medical records, so we haven't any idea if you're on anything."

"Nothing much. A low dose aspirin is all. Don't even care for taking them, but my granddaughter insisted." He looked away, the pain of her death tearing into him. "She was all I had in the world and they killed her."

"She's not dead." Paddy hurt himself turning back to the man. "I don't know what you were told, but a friend of ours has her hidden away. When he was here yesterday, he told me—"

"I was on the phone with her when they shot her. I

heard…you would not believe how many shots I heard. She can't have lived through that." Aedan got up and pulled out his phone and handed it to him. The picture looking back at him wasn't flattering nor was it a good one, but he'd know that face anywhere.

His baby girl. She was bandaged up and had tubes in her, but she was alive. Touching the small screen, he felt his heart break in two knowing that he might have been responsible for her being hurt. When he handed the phone back to the man, he sat there not able to say a word. Aedan seemed to understand.

"She had on a vest. I've been told it was the best on the market by my sister-in-law. Army issue, Storm said. It's more than likely what kept her alive until she could get help. Mason, the man that told you to come here, has her phone as well. I guess she took a great many pictures with it before he took her away." Paddy asked him how she was doing. "I only know that she's in critical condition and that they're doing everything they can for her. And that she's not in the United States. He figured that she'd be safer by not being here until she could be moved back."

"I was told to come here. Well, not to this house but to another one if I was ever on the run or needed to lay low. I only knew to come here when I met up with this Mason person. A vampire. He the one that has her?" Aedan told him it was the same person, and that Storm had told Mason to have Paddy drive to Aedan's house. "I thank you for that. They tried to kill me as well. I'm sure that…what do you know, young man?"

"Nothing. And if you want to know the truth, it's probably less than nothing. I know your name and hers. That she was shot, as were you. And other than her being a cop and shot in the line of duty, that's about it." The short knock at the door had Aedan going to answer it. When the tall man came in holding a tray, Aedan put out a portable table for him to use to eat from. Paddy wasn't sure how much he could eat or even if he wanted to, but he knew that he had to get his strength back or he'd not be able to help his baby girl. "Your guns and other weapons that you had on your person are there in the top drawer of the dresser. The car that you came in, it's been looked over by the best and there are no tracking devices on it at all. The money and other items you had are still in it. Storm said to tell you good job on having it set up. The keys to the car are in the ignition as well."

"Thank you so much. You just never know in our line of work when you might have to skedaddle out of town. But I was wondering if I could use your phone?" Aedan said that he could but he'd rather he didn't. "I have a relative that I need to get in touch with. He'll be able to help out some with all this."

"The president? Howard Wayneright is who you want to call?" Paddy said nothing, and the spoon that he'd only just filled with broth fell to the bowl. "He's been calling me on a burner every couple of hours. And so you know, he's a good friend of my family as well. As I mentioned, Storm Browning is my sister-in-law."

"Well, I'll be cock-doodled." Aedan laughed and Paddy smiled. "Nikki, she said I have a way with putting together words that make her laugh. She's really all right, boy? Don't kid an old man when his family is all he's got."

"I don't know if I'd say she was all right, but according to Mason, she'll live. The vest, as I said before, saved her life." Paddy had spent a small fortune on that thing and was glad now that he had. "I could have hired you a nurse—there was one willing to come here and stay with you—but I was afraid, if you want to know the truth. I didn't want to bring anyone else in that might talk. And Howard, he told me that you and Nikki are the world to him."

"You sound like a man who's got some experience in this sort of stuff. Browning, you said she was your sister-in-law?" He told him she was married to his brother, Riordan. "Just how many of you are there? I know of four already. You, the one you called Darcy, I think, this Riordan person, and Ennis the doctor."

"Six. Six of us boys, as my mom calls us, two sisters-in-law that I'd not fuck with, and my parents. I talked to Storm a few hours ago. Her and Riordan came home last night and she said she'd be over to see you when they were briefed."

Paddy nodded. "I don't have a lot of contact with Howard, not for a lot of years now. It was determined when he started making a name for himself in the political field that we would cut ties. Not so much for him, but to keep the two of us safe. He talks to me, again on a burner, but we don't go out and see him, and Nikki has never met him at all. As I have said, it was safer for all of us." Aedan asked how. "Well, Nikki is undercover. I was as well when I was working before she came along to live with me. So, if we were to show up at a few functions, even one, and have our pictures taken, our careers would be over. And the kind of crappola that we deal with, it's better if we're not associated with a man who can call out the national guard with only a single phone call, don't you think?"

"Yes, I can see that. I never thought of it that way." Paddy nodded and ate more of the broth, which was delicious. "You knew when you got here that I wasn't human. Mason said he never told you. How did you know?"

"About five years before I was to retire, I worked with a

man that was a shifter. He said he was elite. It was the most amazing and terrifying thing in the world working with someone that could be anyone and anything. He showed me a few things that helped me, I guess you could say. And gave me ways of keeping myself safe when it came to a showdown with one. Not that I've had any trouble with any of you shifters, but I guess there are some bad ones out there, like in any race." Paddy eyed Aedan. "Some kind of cat, I would think. And before you tell me I'm wrong, let me tell you how I deduced that. There are no spiders in this house. A home this old, while well maintained, would have a few somewhere. No dogs either. I'm allergic so I can tell they've never been here. And your eye color reminds me of a tiger. Not sure what kind."

"I'm a Bengal. Pureblood too, if that matters to you." Paddy smiled, feeling pretty good about still having it. "I'm impressed. I don't say that often to someone I've only just met. But my brother is here, Riordan. He'd like to have a word with you about your safety and that of this family. Another of my brothers, Mac, his wife is expecting and it's important to all of us that she's safe. Storm? Well, anyone coming here to cause harm had better be more afraid of her than any of us. I'm sure that you know not only what she is but how bad ass she is."

Paddy nodded and said he'd see Riordan now. Aedan left to get him, taking the tray out as he did. Leaning his head back against the seat, Paddy thought about his Nikki. If she really was alive, which he had no doubt now that she was, she'd be a target of any one of the men she'd been working to bring in. He knew one of them personally, and was sure he was looking for her and him as well. He didn't want to get this family into trouble, at least any more than they were in now, but he also knew that he wasn't up to the task of keeping himself safe, much less them.

As soon as the door opened Paddy reached for his sidearm that wasn't there. Looking at the man, Riordan, Paddy thought if anyone could keep him safe while he was laid up, this family would if they were all as big as this one. Christ, he was strong looking too. But when he smiled at him, as he was right now, Paddy could also see the kindness in him, and that made him trust the guy more.

"Mr. Neal? I have word from Mason that your granddaughter is awake and talking. Not much...she's as closed mouthed as my mom at Christmas. But she seems to be on the mend."

Paddy couldn't help it, he cried like a little baby. It was the best news he'd ever had in his life.

CHAPTER 3

Nikki hurt all over. And when she'd asked the doctor how bad it was, he only stared at her for several seconds before he handed her a mirror and let her have a look for herself. She didn't think there was any part of her body that wasn't black and blue right now. And most of that was covered in lines of stitches. The vest had done its job, that was all she could think about right then.

She also had figured out she was no longer in the States, and that she was in a house where a room had been rigged up to be a care unit, and not in a hospital. It had taken her an entire day to figure out just where she was. The South of France didn't sound like it would have been a place she would have been taken when she'd been hurt, but then, who the hell knew anymore? But she wasn't dead, and that was the best news.

"Miss?" Nikki looked at the nurse and said nothing. They'd been coming in every half hour or so and asking her if she remembered her name, which she did, if she knew why she was here, which she wouldn't answer under threat of death, and if she remembered the president of her country's name. That she was sure of. "You have a visitor. May I bring him in to see you?"

"No. I don't know anyone, and I don't want you to bring a stranger in here with me." The nurse smiled at her and moved out of the way of the door, and there stood a stranger. Upon waking, she had found a gun next to her in bed, she pulled it out and pointed it at the man standing there. "I don't know you. What the fuck do you want?"

"No, you do not know me, for the moment anyway. May I have a seat? The sun is too much for me." She nodded and realized that he was a vampire. And more than likely a great deal older than her and the building she was in put together. "Your grandfather sends his love. Well, that's not what he said. He said to tell his baby girl that he has her back. And that come your next birthday the two of you are going on a cruise to see how the underworld really lives, and not this joke here on earth."

It was him. There was no doubt about it. Only the two of them would want to go to the underworld, knowing that they'd been to hell and back too many times for them to count. But Nikki hadn't just fallen off the wool wagon, as her grandda said, so she held the gun on the man.

"Where is he?" He told her he was at a friend's house. "Here? Wherever here is. And that would be my next question, by the way. Where am I and how the fuck did I get here?"

"You are in my home in France, as I believe you have figured out. And I brought you here so that you could be safe. Or as safe as I could make you." She nodded. "This would go so much easier if I did not have to worry that your finger would slip and you'll kill me. Could you please put the gun down? When I brought it to you, I thought you'd feel better. Paddy said that you slept with yours under your pillow."

"I still don't know you." He told her. "Just Mason? No sire name? I find that hard to believe."

The gun was too heavy and she didn't so much put it down as she dropped it. Her entire being felt like he might have drained her and she was still recouping her losses. She asked him if he'd given her his blood.

"No, I was forbidden to. By your uncle. Who sent me, by the way." Uncle Howard. That explained a great deal. "He said that you were very distrusting and for good reason. But for my last name. The deed to this house has Smith on it. If I did have a last name, I have long since forgotten it. At my age, it meant very little to me then and now. And I would prefer that you called me Mason anyway."

"Grandda told me once that to let anyone bite me, for any reason, would give parts of my life away that I'd never get back. And in my line of work, that's not a good thing." Nikki laid back on the pillow. "The men who shot me, do you know if they're looking for me?"

"I do and they are. However, they do believe, like the rest of the department that you worked for, that you are dead. And for now, that is the best way to keep you safe. Your body wasn't recovered, but you left behind just enough blood that no one would think that you could have survived." She nodded, thinking of the day she'd been shot. "You've been under my care for over a week now. Your grandfather, as I mentioned, is awake and doing much better knowing that you're not deceased. I have contacted someone that can let him know that you're awake and seemingly with all your faculties. Are you?"

"That remains to be seen. He was hurt too?" He told her

what had happened. "Do you think I could talk to him? Just long enough to hear his voice? I don't want him to...he's all I have in the world."

"He said as much about you. But I'm afraid, for now anyway, that the two of you have to remain distant from each other. The men that shot you, they're looking for the two of you as we speak, and it would undo all that we've done to keep you both alive if you were to have a long conversation. I don't know what they have in the way of tracers, and while I have some knowledge of phones and what they can do, I'm sure there are others out there that know a great deal more. The people that are watching over him, they're innocent in all of this. Only doing a favor for your uncle." She felt tears fill her eyes when she thought of her grandda being hurt because of her. "What can I tell you so that you don't worry overly much?"

"The men who tried to kill us...do you know if the police are looking for them?" Mason said that they were not doing much of anything as far as he was concerned. "Because the department is dirty. My captain, I'm betting."

"That would be my guess as well. Paddy said that he told you to take James and not go directly home. I think, to hear my friend — his name is Aedan, by the way — but to hear him talking, your grandda might be blaming himself for you being shot. They were there waiting on you, were they not?" She nodded. "He thinks he might have led you right to them."

"No, they knew where I was. Or at least where I was headed. Home. I was on the phone with him when.... I took some pictures. Do you know if they're safe?" He said that the phone was in his lair and no one could get to it. "But is it on?"

"I took the sim card out after making sure that all your pictures were uploaded onto it. Very smart of you to have done that, by the way. Then when it was apparent that you had done that, I destroyed the phone. No one will find the information that you took where it is now." Nikki thanked him and felt her body getting weaker as she laid there. "When you wake again, I'll arrange to bring you some snapshots of Paddy. And I'll take some of you for him when you are less…I was going to say weak, but I think he will not believe me if I were to do that."

"No, he's pretty savvy for an old man, or so he keeps telling me. Are you going to take them now?" He asked if that would be all right. "Yes. But would it offend you if I flipped him off? I mean, it's something that we do."

"No. It will more than likely ease his mind and heart to see that you have your humor still." He pulled out his phone and took several pictures of her. Blowing him a kiss in the last one took a lot out of her, and she laid back. "Now, you should rest. The nurse that has been caring for you is loyal only to me and will never tell anyone where you are, even under threat of death. If it comes to that."

When she was alone, Nikki closed her eyes and willed her body not to hurt. She knew that she was lucky to be alive, and was going to take care that she stayed that way. Just knowing that her grandda was going to be all right as well made her rest easier. She wondered how badly he'd been hurt, and thought of Adkins and his gang that had been there when she'd turned up James.

They weren't expecting her to be where she had been. She knew that now. It hadn't been their plan to take her out with witnesses, and had they been on her street, just one block over, there wouldn't have been any. Even now, she'd bet anything that no one had inquired after the woman that had been shot, nor had they said a word to the police. Adkins was going down for this and a great many other things that she knew about him. Nikki looked at her forearm and wondered if anyone had noticed the deep scar there.

Touching the tiny chip that she'd put there several months before the shooting, she thought of her grandda helping her with the minor surgery. He too, had a matching one in his leg with all the same information on it as hers did. Grandda had said that if anything happened to either of them, then someone would know what to do with the chips, provided that they weren't cut out of them after someone killed them. Nikki doubted anyone that she knew would think to look where they had hidden her files.

Moving as gently as she could to check herself, Nikki felt like she had several broken ribs in addition to the bullets that had not been stopped by her vest. She had been just on the verge of taking the sucker off when she'd talked to Grandda, and was now glad that she'd left it on. Christ, there was little doubt that she would not be alive had she not.

Adkins had been on her radar for months before all this shit had gone down. And the six months that she'd been underground with a small cell of his men had been enlightening, as well as very stressful. Nikki knew that she'd done a good job at slowing down his drugs coming into the city, but not enough to stop the man altogether. That was going to take more. A lot more than what she had right now.

Had she not studied every nuance of the man and the people that worked for him, she was sure that he would have found out long ago where his mole was. It surprised her to no end that her captain, a man that she had figured out was dirty, hadn't turned her over to him. But then, he wasn't very smart, and he thought she was working on a prostitution ring, nothing that Adkins ever dealt with. Over ninety shipments, all of them drugs, had been confiscated at the pickup point before it had hit the houses to be broken down and sold off.

Nikki trusted no one but her grandda, and for good reason, she supposed. She was working with a partner, a handler that she gave information to, but nothing more than a few small time dealers and a couple of meth labs that were about to be closed down anyway.

Mostly it was about the cat houses, the places that would bring in men, fuck their brains out, then take them for all they had. Pictures and video were used to blackmail the men, and most of them, more than half, killed themselves rather than dealing with the fallout.

But the busts of drugs and shipments that she'd been responsible for had been given to her grandda, and he'd handed them off to people he knew. It was why whatever happened never came back to bite her in the ass. It wasn't the cops but the Feds that were getting the kudos. But she could live with that too, so long as that shit was off the streets.

Closing her eyes, she tried not to think about how much she hurt. Not just her body, but her heart as well. She and her grandda had talked a great deal about what would happen in the event that something like this ever come to pass. He was to go away, never to return. She knew that he had enough money and other paperwork to live a good long time. And trusted lawyers to get him her pension as well as her insurance money in the event that she was killed. Which they both knew was highly likely.

Nikki wished that he was here with her now. That he was holding her hand like he had when she was a little girl. And telling her stories about his days as a beat cop working his way up as an FBI agent. Christ, she loved that old man more than she did herself.

~~~

Aedan wasn't sure what to do with his hands. Nor his body, for that matter. Every time someone would walk by him in the television studio, he'd feel like begging them to tell him what to say. But he only had to look down at his hand, the one that his mom had put a small mark on, to know that he was going to be all right. The small magic marker drawn paw print did a lot for his nervousness.

He was going to be in a debate with the current governor… an idiot for sure, but this had been planned without Aedan's knowledge. Aedan had been at his office, the one that he used to work for the Harrison Firm, when his phone buzzed. Picking it up while still reading over the paperwork that he should have turned in yesterday, he barely heard his secretary telling him who was on the other end before telling her it was fine.

"Mr. Harrison, Aedan Harrison?" He sat up in his seat when he heard his name from an unfamiliar voice. "This is Cable News 10. We're wondering what kind of ticket that you're running under, and what you think about the debate tomorrow night."

"Debate?" She laughed and told him that it was tomorrow night on television. Then she proceeded to tell him that her network was carrying it live. "I'm sorry, but I've not been notified of any debate. Are you sure about this?"

She laughed again and he wanted to smack her. Not prone to violence, he had to let out a long breath before he reached out to Riordan to see what he knew about it.

Nothing. Are you sure? He told him what Penelope, the caller, had told him. *Let me do some checking. Can you get her to give you a few minutes?*

I'm sure she won't notice. She's been going on for the last five

*minutes about how her station, Cable 10 by the way, is carrying
all the debates, as well as some Christmas line-up that will knock
your socks off.* Riordan was still laughing when he told him
again to hang on. When she took a breath, Aedan cut her off.
"I'm sorry, but I've not been notified of any debate, and I've
contacted some people, and they knew nothing about it either.
Can you give me some short details on it?"

"You were to be notified by courier a week ago." He told
her he had not been. "I'm sure that I have the receipt here
somewhere. Let me find it on my desk." She asked if he had
signed for it. Aedan told her that he thought he'd remember
something like that. "That's strange. I was just given a list of
names that were going to be there, just you and the governor
it turns out, and to contact you to get information on your
ideas for the state. I have no idea where the receipt is. And it
would only be the one that was attached to it when I took it to
the courier office."

"I don't have anything like that. Who would have set it
up?" She gave him the names of the company that gave her the
short list, and the courier company that they used all the time.
"All right. I need you to hang on for just a moment please."

Without waiting for a reply, Aedan put her on hold
and called out to Cindy and asked her to check on it. In two
minutes she had answers for him. He leaned back in his chair
and tried to think.

The letter had never left the courier's office. It still sat,
sealed and ready to go out, on the desk of the man who was
supposed to bring it to him. When Cindy tried to get someone
to tell them why Aedan had never gotten it, they replied that
they were told to wait until tomorrow to deliver it. Not a week
ago, but the day of the event. Someone didn't want him to
have any information on this.

It's in the papers that there is a debate, but no mention of who it might be with. And it might have been on the television, but as you know, we don't watch much of it. He didn't either and told Riordan what he'd only just found out. *They're making you look bad, and as a no-show, which I'm sure is what he's hoping for, he'll be able to bash you without you there to say differently.*

Yeah, that's what I'm thinking as well. Do you suppose that the person setting this up, or me up, in this is someone that works for Ellison? Riordan said he'd count on that. *I have to get ready. I mean, he's going to throw questions at me and I need to have answers.*

I'm sure that you'll do fine. Aedan wasn't so sure. He wasn't one to go into things without plenty of planning. *Just write up what you want to say and be calm. Come over tonight and I'll help you out if you want. But you're going to do fine.*

After closing the connection with Riordan with the promise of going over after he saw to his guest, he picked up the phone to talk to Penelope. He wasn't sure what to tell her about the mess up, so didn't mention what he'd found out. He did, however, get the times and places that he was to be, and cut her off again. He started working on his platform as soon as he finished up the report for Mac.

And now, here he was about to go on television for the first time in his adult life to talk to a man that he had no more respect for than he did the lowest form of scum. It had been a real eye-opener finding the things that Ellison had promised before in his campaign and just how little of it he'd done. Aedan had also come up with ideas of his own, things he was going to follow through on. Jobs for one. And that was in the works now.

At ten minutes before the hour he was introduced to Dewey Ellison. He'd met the man before, talked to him about things that he'd been noticing around the town, and had been fobbed off like he had been about the debate. Ellison seemed genuinely surprised to see him there.

"I wasn't sure that you'd make it. Heard that you've been having a good old time getting your new house in order." Aedan just smiled. He wasn't going to get into that kind of debate with the man about where he lived. "Usually these things get a little heated. The people seem to like it when those running against me give them a good show. Are you up for that, young man?"

"I've watched all your debates, Ellison. I'm sure that this one will be different." He asked him how. "You can't think I'm going to give you all my answers, do you?"

"No, no. Not at all. Like I said, they like a good show and I try and give it to them. I saw your ad with the president. How much did it set you back to have the big guy endorse you? Either that or you had some big time dirt on him." Ellison poked at him, like they'd shared a good joke. "You might want to share that with me when this is all over. Come on over to the governor's mansion. I'll show you around so you can see what you'll be missing. It's a lovely home, by the way. Maybe someday you'll be able to stay there. After I'm done with it, anyway."

"You think?" Ellison just glared at him. "And it's my understanding that we can live where we want, so long as there is security around. I think my house, which I believe is a little larger than the governor's place, will do me just fine."

They were called into the studio to set up, and Aedan was sure that he was going to throw up. But looking out into the people there, he saw his mom. When she blew him a kiss and gave him a thumbs up, Aedan felt calmer. Even his cat seemed to settle down. If he could get out of this with just making a fool of himself and not his family, he might do all right just being a recluse at home from now on.

For an hour and a half, Aedan fielded questions and cut Ellison to the bone. Each time Ellison brought up something, mostly things from the survey that had been sent to Darcy, Aedan was able to come back with a fluent straight answer. He was going to send Storm a dozen roses when this was over for telling him to be prepared for those questions. Aedan smiled to himself when he glanced over at Ellison.

His tie had been loosened to the point that you could now see his jowl. It wasn't hot in the little area, but he was sweating like he was on a desert island without water or breeze. Every time he picked up his notes, ones that were now smeared with sweat, he chuckled about how the lighting was dimmed and that he wasn't sure who had written them out for him.

Aedan hadn't brought notes to the podium that they were standing in front of. They'd made him nervous, and Riordan said that he fussed with them too much when he'd been practicing. Nor did he have any little cheats written on his hands other than the little drawing. His paw print, for as small as it was, helped him in big ways. All he had in front of him was an untouched glass of water. He looked at Storm and she nodded. It was time to hit Ellison where it counted. Aedan cleared his throat when he was given the floor.

"Last time you ran Governor, you mentioned that you were going to bring more jobs to the state. That you'd be taking on tighter control of drugs in the schools, as well as some improvements to the state roads." Storm handed him the file that she had in her hand. Aedan pulled out the first sheet; it was bright yellow. She called it the sunshine sheet because Aedan was going to shove this information where the sun never shined in the governor's body.

"Let me look at my notes here and get the numbers—"

Aedan cut Ellison off. It was his turn and he'd not asked a question of the man yet. "Unemployment is at an all-time high for the state. There are — "

"There has been a downturn in the economy if you remember there, young Harrison. Things don't improve unless I have to raise taxes, and I won't do that to the people who voted me in." He laughed a little. "I'm thinking you have to get a little more knowledge under your belt before you take on this kind of office."

Not a sound was heard from the audience, just the small nervous laughter from Ellison.

"I would appreciate it if you didn't cut me off when I'm speaking. Taxes have gone up four percent. Not a lot if you think of the single person paying that on their homes, but overall it was just over six million and some change. That money was earmarked, you said when you raised the taxes, to go to road improvement projects. So far, not one dollar has gone there." Aedan pulled out another sheet of paper in the stack, this one bright blue. She called this her once in a blue moon paper. He'd only have to say this once to get people thinking. "Unemployment is at an all-time high, as I said, at nearly thirteen percent in some counties. Up nearly four percent since you promised more jobs. There is also — "

"I think you have the wrong information." Aedan looked at him, hoping that he'd say something, anything that he'd be able to catch him on. "I'm sure that your information is a little outdated. Perhaps I can get a better understanding and send the information to that new house of yours."

"I've asked you already not to cut me off. It's my turn to speak, Ellison. And you keep bringing up my home. Once backstage and now here. Do you have a problem with someone being able to afford their first home?" Ellison stuttered around a moment. "You did say in your last campaign that you'd make housing more affordable and bring in more grants, and help with that from the government grants that you could get for our state. So have you since changed your mind about that?"

"No. No, that's not what I said. What I was trying to point out is.... What I meant to say was that you.... Your family comes from a long line of money. Just where did it come from?" Aedan looked at his dad when he stood up, but Riordan pulled him back down before he said anything. "I mean, you should see the things my constituents are saying about you."

"I have." He pulled out the thick stack of questions that his brother had given him over a week ago. "You should be more careful who gets these. And some of these questions that you sent out, they might be considered lies."

"Lies? I never...where did you get that? That was to go out to a certain list.... I don't know what you're talking about."

The audience started screaming questions at them both. Most of them were directed at Ellison about the questionnaire, but Aedan answered a few of his own. But when he lifted his hand up when he was told there were only a few minutes left, the entire room grew deadly quiet. Aedan looked into the camera in front of him.

"Plans are in the works now to bring seven thousand jobs to this state by the end of next year. I, my family, and others have been working on that for several weeks now. Also, there is ample money in the state programs to help lower income people to afford their first homes. In addition to that, if you call my campaign office, you can be directed to websites that can show you where you can get aide in the form of down payments, student loans, and other moneys that have been earmarked for such things." He gave the address and phone number for them to call. "This has nothing to do with votes or with either of us being the governor. It's money that is there to be used to help better your lives and our state, and I'd like to make sure that you know where to find it."

As soon as he was told it was clear, he moved past the people there and headed to the bathroom. Aedan was barely in the stall before he bent at the waist and threw up. Christ, he wasn't sure he was cut out for this shit. Standing up, he leaned against the stall door, then heard the bathroom door open and close, and knew who it was. His dad. Flushing the commode, he went to the sink.

"I don't know if I ever told you this, but you're very scary when you want to be." He looked at his dad in the mirror as he washed up. "You took him right out of the running, I'm thinking. Jiminy Cricket, boy, you only had a day to prepare. I'd hate to see you when you're not hard pressed to get things done. You'll have him before a firing squad by sunset."

"Thanks Dad." Aedan was pulled into a huge bear hug and hugged his dad right back. "Thank you. Thank you for being the best dad that anyone could ever have. I love you."

"I love you too, son. Now get on out there and show them what a Harrison looks like when he's just won the governorship." Aedan laughed with his dad and went out. He'd been wrong thinking his dad was having fun with him. Every person who had been in the seats in front of them was now asking questions. Aedan felt his belly churn up again but stood his ground.

He might have even enjoyed all the attention. Just a little, anyway.

CHAPTER 4

"I think I might have found something." Otis looked at Joe when he came barging into his office. He was afraid it was his wife again. She and his little girl had been coming in here three times a day since the flower crisis. He'd finally told them that if they entered again, he was going to take their credit cards and cars and be done with the lot of them. That had worked better than he'd thought it would. "I've been looking at some footage, something that the police have set up for Amber alerts or something. Here, can you put this in your computer? Anyway, I have Paddy moving down a street on foot. Then I think in a car about six blocks away."

Otis took the small thumb drive from Joe but was so excited to have something, anything, that he fumbled it a few times. Finally, Joe took it back and slid it in where it would work properly. Neither of them mentioned it and Otis was glad. He'd have hated to kill the man after all this time.

"I thought his car was in the garage." Joe said that it was, just as the cameras started where the man was walking down a sidewalk holding his side. The car was as of an hour ago; it had never moved. When the car was stopped at a light somewhere, it was obvious to him that it was Paddy Neal. "Then he had a stash somewhere. Not to mention, if he had a stash set up with a car he might have also had a place to go that no one would have known about. Cash, he would have had cash there as well. That would explain the lack of use of his credit cards too."

"Other than the direction he was headed, I don't know much right now. But I have some clues. Not on the girl, but if we find him, then she'll come out. They're pretty tight, or so I've been told."

Otis knew that as well. He wished at times that he had that sort of relationship with his kid. From some of the reports that he'd read about Nikki and her grandda, the two of them had something special.

Dorothea was just too used to having it all, and he'd come to realize that hadn't just been his fault. Savannah had been just as indulgent. But he figured that if he had it, she should as well. It was coming back to bite him in the ass.

Otis looked at Joe when he realized he'd missed something, and asked him to repeat it.

"We have him on the interstate at about ten the morning we went to talk to him regarding Nikki. The same system picked him up later at a gas station about ten miles from a little town in Ohio. There's an airport there with no kind of camera system, but I don't think he would have used that. But there are any number of places that he could have stopped at to get help."

"Could he have gone on? I mean, the coast is where I would go." Joe shook his head. "Where is he then?"

"I know that he didn't go any further on the interstate

than when he got off at the gas station. I've watched the video myself four times to be sure. He went there and didn't enter the highway onramps again. There is a chance that he took back roads to somewhere—Ohio has a shit load of them—but in his condition, I don't think so. I've already sent out a team to look into doctors and hospitals in the area. He has a minimum of three bullets in him I think, so if he made it that far, he's going to be hurting bad. If not dead."

"Christ, at this point I don't want him dead until I kill him." Joe smiled. "Can you go out there for me? I need you here, but you going there would be better so that I know that it's not going to get fucked up again. Once you find him, call me on my cell and I'll come out. I want this over with. I have a feeling that wherever that bitch is, she's just making her plans to drop a big bowl of shit right over my parade."

He'd lost two more shipments over the last three days. Before he'd had her in his sights, he was sure that someone else was giving up the information, and they were going to pay when he caught them. And he would have. Then two weeks before the big showdown, he'd found out that Nikki's grandfather had been a fucking Fed while he'd been away, and that had to be it. That explained to him who was giving information about his drops.

It wasn't coming through his contact. Well, nothing was now. The man was now at the bottom of the deepest lake Otis knew of. But what bothered him the most was that the fucking bitch wasn't even getting any kind of pay from her department for the collars. She had been giving them over to the big guys, the fucking Feds. Not that anyone would have given her any kind of kudos anyway, at least not the cops he'd had working for him.

What burned his ass was that she'd been able to get in

anyway. For six months she'd been working in some of his labs, going to work every fucking day, and even getting paid with his hard earned money. It had taken him nearly the entire time she was infiltrating his shit for someone to realize in the station house that she might be the one interfering with his work, not one of his own men. Then, once her picture started going around and five people confirmed that they knew her, Otis had killed three of his men before he was able to get his temper under control again.

"I'll drive out today." Otis nodded at Joe. But when he didn't move, Otis looked at the only person in the world that he called friend. "Robert wants to go. I think, like you, he's heard enough about the wedding. You should also know that I don't like him. Don't know why yet, but there is something off about him that makes me want to draw my gun and blow his fucking head off."

"He's been having that same effect on me too. I think it's the stress. At least that's what I'm hoping. But this wedding? You think he's backing out?" Joe shrugged. "Christ, I hope not. Even if you don't count all the money I've poured into this fucking thing, I won't be able to stand either of them if he does. I love my little girl to death, but she might be about the whiniest person I know other than her mother. I need this wedding to go on."

"I'll take him with me. He can make up any kind of excuses he wants to his bride to be. But I draw the line at her coming with us. I can't be around her that long." Otis didn't even think of what he was saying as an insult to her. Dorothea was hard to be around on her best days. And Savannah was about ten times worse. "We'll leave as soon as he can get packed. I've already made arrangements at one of the hotels just outside of the town where Paddy got gas."

After he left him, Otis looked at the thumb drive that Joe had shown him again. Pausing it on the face at the light, he looked at the man. Christ, Otis knew that Paddy was old enough to be his own father, yet he looked like he was more fit than he was. Otis looked down at his expanding waistline and decided that he was going to be slimmer for this wedding. He was not going to be one of those fat fucks that waddled their daughter down the aisle with an oxygen tank simply because he was too lazy to push away from the table in time.

Pulling a file from the bottom of his desk, he took out the only picture he had of Nikki. Sitting it by her grandfather's image, Otis could see that they were related. He wished now that he'd thought about it before it had gotten this far, if he had he might not be in the shit he was in now. As it was, he was losing money on his business, and the woman had more dirt on him than even her grandda had had back in the day. He wondered what else besides his books she had.

Each place that she'd been at the computers had been cloned. Nine of his most profitable labs and distribution centers had to be closed down because of her snooping where she had no business. But by the time he'd found out, it had been too late for some of them. She had enough information to not only bury him, but five more of the bigwigs in town too. He'd been stupid and clumsy in using real names rather than a code. And if they ever found out, the ones on his books, he might as well put the gun to his temple and pull the trigger himself. It would be much quicker and less painful if he did.

Four bank managers who made his money clean were on that list. There was his investment guru that had made sure that all the right paperwork was used to have his money in safe accounts. The county law, the state boys, and a few other highly profiled men and women were on his lists as well, two of them judges that made more money just from making one ruling in his favor than the state paid them for a single year.

These people didn't have much on him; very little, other than that they took bribes from him. But if one fell, it would be like a house of cards. He'd be in prison before the last one got their turn at trying to get a deal from the local and federal crime agencies. This was why Otis hadn't even told Joe of what Nikki had gotten.

It was nearly four later that afternoon when he got a call from Joe. He'd tracked Paddy to a town called Nashport. Beyond that, there wasn't a single hit, not even someone saying he might think he maybe saw him.

"I'm going to see what I can find out in the hospital here. They're remodeling, so it might be easier than I thought to get somewhere. Also, there is a list of doctors here that I'm having Robert check on. Most of them are gynos anyway, but we're still looking." He asked him if Robert was bitching. "Yes. The wedding is in peril, so you know. I guess Dorothea told him that if she didn't get things her way all the time, she'd come running to you and you'd make it right. Also, I think....Well, you might be surprised to know that he has been talking to your wife too. He seems too comfortable around her to me. He's more uptight about the fact that Savannah is upset than he is about his intended."

"My wife? Perhaps I can have a talk to her about it. Maybe she's egging the two of them on or something. But you tell him once he says the right words and doesn't beat her, I'm never stepping in. The house I'm getting them is a wedding present in both their names, and he's already signed the pre-nup, so that's taken care of." Joe said he mentioned that too. "He want out of that?"

"I'm not sure. I've set someone to look into his finances. I think he might be having a few issues of his own." Otis said he'd look from here. "Good. I was wondering how I was going to set that up. Anyway, when I find something on this end, I'll call you, day or night."

"Yes. Be sure that you do." Just before he was ready to hang up, he thought of something else. "This vamp you mentioned. You think he's there? In the town with them? I mean, there can't be that many in such a small ass town, do you think?"

"I'll check. But I would say not. This is a sports town, if you know what I mean. And they have gun racks in the back of their trucks, which everyone seems to drive." Podunk was the first word that popped into Otis's head. "I'm going over to the hospital now, and then in the morning I'm going to check on locals. I'd think he'd stand a better chance of getting one of them to help an old man out than a hospital."

Otis looked at the picture of the man he'd printed out from the surveillance video he'd been given, and wanted to tell Joe to look in the gyms while he was at it. After they closed the connection between them, he put the phone in the cradle only to have it ring again. Picking it up, he figured that it was Joe again.

"What have you found out about the girl?" It took his mind a moment to realize who was on the other end. "You said you'd have something by now. And I don't know if you're aware of this or not, but I think she might have taken our pictures while we were standing there ready to blast her out of the fucking planet."

"I wasn't aware of that. Are you sure?" The man snarled at him that he was. "I've got my best men working on this. We still have no idea what might have happened to her body."

Otis jerked the phone from his ear when Wendell started

cursing. If he knew the half of what shit was going on, he'd be running out of the country. Otis might too before this was all done but for the wedding of the year.

"You find her, I want to know about it. And if I hear on the news or the paper that I'm being indicted, I'm dropping everything at your door." The phone slammed down and Otis just sat there. Calling Joe back, he told him that it was time to end their relationship with Wendell Householder. By this time tomorrow, the man would be dead.

~~~

Ennis was just leaving his office when someone pulled into the parking lot. He was ready to tell them that he was closed up for the day when he looked at them. Everything in him told him to shift and kill them. Calming his cat, he smiled at the men and asked them what he could do for them. It was then that the bigger of the two men made sure that Ennis could see his gun. Fuck.

"We were just checking some things out and were directed to your office to see if you knew anything. We're inquiring about someone that you might have had come here about a week ago. Elderly gentleman that might or might not be shot." He flashed him his badge, and Ennis was able to see that it was from Illinois and nothing more. "We've traced him this far, but so far no one has seen him."

"Do you have a picture of him?" He said that sadly he'd left it in his hotel room. "I don't know that I can help you anyway. I see only a few regulars here right now. I've only just opened my own practice. Before that I worked at a larger firm where people were coming and going so quickly that I'd more than likely take care of my mom and not know it until later."

They both laughed, but the younger man moved up on

the step with him and looked in the window of his offices. The older man, the one with the gun, said nothing, but Ennis could tell that he wasn't happy about whatever it was the younger one was doing. Ennis reached for Riordan.

I have two men here looking for Mr. Neal. They've not said his name nor do they have a picture, but they're from Illinois. I think they're trying to pose as good old boys, but the younger of the two is antsy and making my cat pissy. Riordan asked if he was alone. *Yes. I'm not in my offices but out in the empty parking lot. Are you close?*

No, but I don't think you're going to like who is on their way. Ennis closed his eyes. It was either Storm or his dad, neither of which was going to help. Storm would shoot first and talk later. His dad would just want to ask too many questions, and that would get them both killed. *Dad and Storm are about there. I didn't send them, but Dad wanted to see your new digs and Stormy was with him. Sorry buddy. You might want to kill them both before they get there; it might be less painful.*

They're armed. At least one of them is. He asked him if he thought Stormy wasn't. *True. But if it's all the same to them, can you just tell them for now it's only a friendly conversation? Not a die or be killed sort of one.*

He could see them then. His dad was talking like he always did, his arms going a mile a second, telling a story that he'd more than likely told a million times. Stormy was nodding, but he knew the exact moment she got the information from Riordan. She paused and his dad stopped to look in their direction. As soon as his dad peeled away and headed to the store across the street, Ennis felt a little better, but not much. Stormy was still coming.

"Boys?" They both turned to look at Stormy. The older man just nodded, but the younger one seemed to take her question as an invitation to get closer. Ennis might have warned him not to bother, she was happily married to his brother, but thought this would be fun. "Something we can help you with?"

"You a doctor too?" She told the younger man she was Ennis's sister. "Sister? Damn, but they sure do grow women well around Ohio, don't they? Please tell me that you like to have a good time, and this might be a match made in heaven."

When he put out his hand to touch her, just her shoulder, Ennis had to cover his mouth as even before the man could take his next breath, Storm had his arm up behind his back and he was down on his knees in front of her. The man was cursing like a sailor and Stormy was just smiling as she continued questioning the other man. He just shook his head as if he'd seen this fool in this position before.

"I wanted to know if we can help you. You see, we're sort of the welcoming committee around these parts, and well, we don't take well to being mauled by strangers." The other man laughed too and said he was sorry. "Thank you. I never dreamed that all those self-defense lessons would pay off so quickly. Did you?"

When she asked him and winked, he laughed again. "No, I surely didn't. And if you break his arm, I'm to understand you get extra points toward your black belt, is that right?"

"I think you might be right." Storm pulled just hard enough for his arm to move out of the socket. He heard the sound and knew that the man had to be in a great deal of pain, both now and when it was set again. She looked at the other man. "You might need to take him someplace else. I'm thinking another city than here. What do you think?"

"I think we were just leaving." The younger man was released, and just as he lunged at Storm, she pulled her gun out and simply put it by her side. Neither man moved, but the older one said, "We don't want any trouble."

"You should have thought of that before he touched me." The man nodded. "It's past time you left."

As they were pulling out of the parking lot, Ennis stood near Storm. He waved at the car when the younger man flipped them both off. He turned to her when they were out of sight.

"We're in deep shit." She nodded, but didn't move. "They might not have known before that he was here, but I'm pretty sure they know now. Not because of you, but I think that older man is smarter than the younger."

"The cat that hangs out in the barn at the house is smarter than he is. Did you see the way he puffed out his chest? As if that is supposed to be sexy. Christ, men only think with one thing, their twig and berries." He laughed when she did. "We'll have to bring her here now. Gather the wagons so to speak. If they got this far with nothing more than what little brains they have, it won't be long before they find Mason too. After that, it's only a simple search to see where his lairs are."

"You think they're that smart?" She told him to never underestimate the stupidity of criminals. "I guess you're right. But is she healthy enough to move?"

"I don't know that it matters. And if she finds out that they know he's here, from what I've heard about her, she'll come running with or without our help. Her grandda is her world." Ennis knew that as well. "I'll contact Mason. The sooner we get our shit together, the better. To be honest, I'm surprised it took them this long to figure this out."

He was too. Walking to the Bakery where his dad was, he told them what he knew. Stormy was in the back room, and he had a feeling that Mason would be moving to get the woman sooner than they could get a plane to get her. It might be safer for her if he did it his way anyway. Planes, even a jet as they had, would require paperwork. And that would be just what they needed to find them both.

Aedan would have to be warned as well. Soon too. Either Mr. Neal would have to be moved again, or the girl was going to want to stay there with him. Ennis did not envy his brother. Aedan was about to have his entire world shook up. He laughed; more than likely the whole family was going to hear about it too. He decided to stir the pot while he waited on his family to come to the Bakery to decide what to do.

What do you mean, someone is looking for him? I was told that no one would find him. Ennis pointed out that they were two different things all together. *I know that, moron. What I meant was, why him and not her? I thought she was the one they were after. You know, I have no idea what is going on. There is at this moment, while very nice, a stranger living with me, who has a granddaughter that was shot up by someone, and she's somewhere no one knows but a vampire that can't come....*

When his brother stopped ranting, Ennis stood up. Something had happened, he knew it. He was about out the door when he heard from his brother again. This time his voice was tight and cold.

Come to my house, please. It seems I have another houseguest. And apparently she didn't take the transfer here as well as one would hope. Also, you will not believe what she is. Before he could ask, Aedan spoke again. *My fucking mate has just arrived in my bedroom, the only other bed in the house, mind you, and she's cursing worse than Storm does when she's in a snit.*

Ennis told him he was on his way, but he supposed he should have stopped laughing before he did that. Aedan was still calling him names and threatening him with bodily harm when he walked back to his offices and got his bag. This might be the best fun he'd had in a very long time. Ennis was just glad that it was happening to his brother and not him.

Stopping by the Bakery to get a lift because he'd walked to work, he let Stormy and Riordan know what was going on. They, of course, said they were coming with him. Aedan was not going to be any happier with that information than he was with his new guest.

They were all still laughing when they pulled up in front of the gatehouse. The large barrel of a man there asked for their identifications, and then called up to the house to gain entrance. He was a bear shifter, Ennis realized when he handed him his license. While he was glad that Aedan was taking care that he was safe, he couldn't help be a little annoyed about having to wait…until Stormy spoke from the seat across from him.

"How did it feel to have those men come up on you without you knowing what they were about?" He told her that he'd been a little nervous and somewhat scared. "Yeah, I bet. Think about how Aedan feels now. He not only has a mate up there, but her grandfather as well. Add to that salad a man that might be out to kill her, and the number of crazies that you know are going to be happy to pounce on him every time he leaves the house because of the shit the other night."

"You think that'll happen?" She said she was sure of it. "Would any of them by chance be Ellison? I don't think he's too happy about the debate the other night either."

"He won't dirty his hands. But I don't think he's above getting someone else's dirty to get a job done." Ennis asked her if she thought he'd kill his brother. "No. Not kill, but I don't think I'd turn my back on him if I were Aedan. Or any of us for that matter. He's going to play dirty because he has nothing truthful to go on right now."

Ennis decided that he needed to take better care of his place as well. When these men came here, and there was little doubt that they would now, he wanted to not be caught unawares again. He also decided that lessons in carrying a gun and how to use it might be needed. Even if he never encountered these men himself, Aedan might very well be president someday, and there would be a lot more crazies to deal with.

CHAPTER 5

"You most certainly will not be helping to keep us safe. I can do that well enough on my own." Aedan scrubbed his hand over his face. The woman, Nikki, was making things much more difficult than they needed to be. And he was sick to death of her talking to him like he was an idiot. "Now, here is what is going to happen. You're going to pack my grandda up and we're going to find us someplace to lay low. You will also not be calling in any more people to protect us so that they can be hurt. And that idea where you want us in separate rooms even if we stayed isn't going to fly either. And you most assuredly will not be trying to tell me what to do again."

"But it's all right for you to tell me what to do. In my own house, I might add." She crossed her arms over her chest and he wanted to shake her. But he didn't move any closer to her. The last time he'd done that, she'd nearly put his balls up around his ears. "Look, all I suggested, and that is all I did, was that you lie down until my brother gets here to have a look at you. I can see how much pain you're in. Why don't you just sit down and — ?"

"I am not yours to order around." He'd had enough. Stomping toward her, he pushed her back until she fell in the bed behind her. And before she could get up, as there was no doubt that she might, he put his hands on her shoulders and his knee on her legs so she couldn't kick him again.

"This is me ordering you around, not what I was doing before. Now, if you so much as look like you're going to get up from this bed, I will find something to tie you here with. And so help me, as fun as that sounds about now, I don't think you'd enjoy it as much as I'd like for you to with you bleeding like you are."

Moving his hands down her arms, he felt her shudder. Christ, she was beautiful. Even spitting mad like she was, all he wanted to do was lean into her body and taste any part of her that she'd let him. Which he was betting wouldn't be as much as he wanted. When he leaned down into her neck, just to see if she really did smell as good as he'd thought, she jerked him up by his hair and tumbled him off her. Only instead of him hitting the floor as she might have thought, he was still on the bed and she was now over him.

Every part of him knew what she was to him. Not just a woman, and Christ that was obvious enough, but his mate too. Even his cat, who lately had seemed to not want anything to do with him, perked up. Running his hands up her thighs to her hips, Aedan rocked up into her. He wanted her, and he was pretty sure that she knew it.

"Should we come back?" Aedan felt his body freeze, his hand tightening at her waist. He'd been so close to seeing if her breasts were as full as they looked when Riordan spoke from the doorway. "Aedan, did you know that she's bleeding?"

He rolled her to her back and stood up. But not before

rocking into her again. When she moaned, it was all he could do not to tell his family to go away. Backing from the bed, he stood near her while Ennis and Storm came into the room with Riordan. He found Paddy in the hall, leaning heavily on the table there with a gun in his hand.

"You should be resting. I told you that you did too much yesterday."

He helped the man to the bedroom where he'd been staying until Ennis was done patching Nikki up and could check on him too. When Aedan helped him into the chair, the man reached for his hand, and it was all he could do not to snatch it back from him. Paddy must have heard the low growl and looked up at him.

The stare might have made him uncomfortable if he wasn't already embarrassed and out of sorts. He let the man look as deeply as he wanted. Aedan had come to like the man and respected him, and didn't want him to be afraid of him.

"She's my mate. I don't need a mate right now messing with my plans." Paddy nodded and smiled. "I have my life all planned out. Things like a mate will only make it difficult to see them to the end."

"I see. And this life you planned out to the letter, what happens if something like this puts a monkey wrench in it? You gonna have a hissy fit and crawl in a corner?" Aedan told him he had no idea. "I'm pretty sure, and this is just me as a human, but once you find your mate, I think it's pretty much all cocked up, don't you?"

"Yes. That's about as apt a word for it as you can find." Aedan sat down on the bed. "I'm running for governor, as you know. I don't have time to court a woman, make her understand what I want from her, and try and keep my head above water in this extra work I'm putting myself in. A mate is not in the plans for another year or more."

"I see. So this would be about how it doodles up your plans and what you have to do to make Nikki comply with them. I want you to know right now, that isn't gonna fly with her. I'm sure you'll come to understand right quick that she doesn't take orders well, and if you think you can get her to obey....Well, you might want to get you a dog; you'd have better luck getting it to mind you. She won't settle with that no matter how you try and pretty it up." Yeah, Aedan was afraid of that too. "Tell you what. The first time you try and get her to bend to your way of thinking, you let me know."

"So you can be there to make fun of me when I'm made to look like a fool?" Paddy shook his head. "Then you think she'll listen and be reasonable?"

"No. I want to know so that when she draws out her piece and shoots you in the last part of you jumping the fence, I have time to run and hide. A man my age and shot up, I need a little extra time to hide when the shit hits the fan." He was still laughing when Aedan made his way to the door. But he stopped him before he left his ass there with his humor. "Aedan, there can be worse things in life to mess around with your plan than a wife. While my Nikki is a little rough and carries a gun for a living, she's loyal, loving, and about the best person I know."

"I'm sure that's all true. But this job and running for the office? I'm not sure that I would be able to devote any time to her and her needs."

"Her needs? Boy, what do you think she's going to need that you can't simply give her by loving her? You'll see. It'll turn out just fine as rain water in a barrel."

Aedan went out in the hall, and he could still hear the man laughing. He started down the hall but decided to go to the kitchen first. He was having some updates made, and Winnie had asked to speak to him before all of this shit happened. He nearly left when he saw his mom and dad in there.

"You come here and give me a hug, young man." He hugged his mom and shook his dad's hand. "Your brother told us that this Nikki person is your mate. Is she sweet? Oh, I hope so. And a cop too. How lucky are you?"

He wanted to tell her that he wasn't lucky. Nor was he happy. But he was pretty sure that they could see that. Instead of letting them ask him what was going on, he grabbed his keys and left the house. Whatever was going on, and there was plenty, someone else could take care of it for a little while.

Walking by his car, he went to the woods behind the garage instead. He was pretty sure that if he ran fast enough, and for long enough, that his problems might not be there when he returned. Yes, and as Paddy was so fond of saying, hanging out the wash in the rain don't make them any dryer. He wasn't sure what that meant really, but he wasn't sure of too much of anything at the moment.

Stripping down to his bare skin, he took off to the trees. Running as his animal was something that he didn't get to do as much as he wanted, and he thought he might at least have better control of his temper when he got back if he did.

Aedan had been gone for about an hour when he came upon the fast moving creek that ran about midway through his land. He'd been told that it flooded in the spring but didn't reach the house, which he was happy to hear. He had already decided to have it dug a little deeper. He had plans to put a barn back here, and that would be hurt if the creek came up too high. He closed his eyes and laid down for a moment.

"I'm coming up to your left and from behind you, Aedan." He didn't stand when Andi spoke to him. It was on the tip of his tongue to tell her to go away, but she'd been so sweet to him that he felt horrible about saying anything bad to her. Besides, being pregnant like she was, she would cry at the strangest things. "Can I have a seat with you? I promise I won't ask you any questions."

Sure. Go ahead. But tell me which one sent you out here. She told him no one, she'd been out and about and saw him and decided to have a nice sit down. *Did Mac tell you I found my mate? Or she found me, I guess.*

"Yes. I heard about it." She leaned against him and closed her eyes. "I saw the doctor today. He said that I'm doing just fine. He also gave me a book to read. I had no idea what to expect when I saw the cover. But I read it. I think it made me have more questions than it answered anything. It's mostly about the changes in my body that will be going on over the next several months."

Mom will be able to help you if you don't want to ask the doctor. She said she'd think on it. *You can't be doing this for a while, walking around without protection. There are some people out there trying to kill Nikki. That's her name…my mate is Nikki Neal.*

"I know. I have a gun, but I kinda of knew that you'd be out here. I heard that you had left your house and figured you'd be here." He wanted to snap at her that he didn't like people talking about him behind his back, but he only lay there. He wasn't even sure what he was angry about really. He couldn't care less if he was the topic of conversation usually. "I was trying to think what to get Mac for Christmas. Your mom said that anything I got him would be great. But I want it to be special. This is our first Christmas together, and I want it to be memorable."

I think I can help you with that. Did you know that Mac collects pottery? She said that she had seen his collection. *My mom said that he was having it moved to your home after the holidays. I guess it's grown quite a bit since he was living with us all. I know that he takes a great deal of pride in it.*

"We're having a room set up for it in the back of the house. I mean, we're having one built off the back of the house. As if the house isn't big enough for me to get lost in. Anyway, he said that he started collecting when he was about nine, when your mom picked him up a piece when they were on vacation somewhere." He told her that they'd been in the Smokey Mountains. "That's right. It was made by a local potter, I guess, and he loved it so she got it for him."

The man let him play on the wheel. I don't think Mac ever got the hang of it, but he did enjoy the form and the way it had to be done. I remember the older man being very patient with him too. I'm not sure, but I think Mac might have taken a few lessons when he was older. In college, I think. Andi said that he had. *What I was getting at is that there is this potter that he loves. His name is Rickson, I think. He's from someplace down south. Anyway, this potter has this beautiful raku stuff that Mac's been coveting for years. I think he has one or two pieces by the artist. I don't know why he's never gotten any more of it, but you might try looking for that.* She said that she would look.

They sat there for a little while longer, neither of them saying anything else, listening to the creek as it made its way to something larger and deeper. Aedan felt at peace for the first time in a long while.

"Will it be so bad?" He knew what she was asking him, and since he was feeling pretty good, he told her it would. "I see. Because of your plans."

Do you know how hard it is to juggle this work and that of the family business and keep them going? What I'm doing right now is all I can handle for the moment. Do you know how much everyone is going to be looking into every single part of my life from now on? She said that she didn't, but imagined that he would be just fine and get it all done. *Yes, I will, but it will take me longer now that I have someone to watch out for. It's messing with my timeline, having someone like a mate come along.*

"You think you will? Have to watch out for her, I mean. I heard from Stormy that this woman is a highly decorated officer, and has been asked several times to join the FBI to help them out." Figures, more things for him to have to worry about. "I don't suppose you ever thought of what this is going to do to her, did you?"

What do you mean, to her? I'm the one that is taking a mate. I'm the one that's going to have to change everything I've worked for over the last year and a half. Hell, most of my life. She laughed and he felt his peace evaporate just like that. *I don't see how this is the least bit funny, Andi.*

"Don't you? I do. You were never like this, this selfish, when I first came here. I can understand why you didn't fuss when Stormy came to your family. She's scary even when she's in a good mood. But you just went along with me being a part of this family too, didn't you?" He asked her what she meant by that. And when she stood up, he did as well. "I messed with your plans, didn't I? I mean, I came to this family for a job and security. Who knew that I was going to have to murder two people to get it? One of them was my aunt. And I had a very good friend killed too. Was that in your flow charts and pies?"

No. And I don't think you're thinking of this from my point of view. I have a mate now that is going to need things from me that I just don't have time to deal with. Andi smacked him on the end of his nose and he saw stars. *What the fuck was that for?*

"That's for being childish. And I should hit you again for being a jackass. Yes, you're a jackass. Let the great and powerful Aedan Harrison tell you his woes while his mate, new to this family, lies up in a stranger's bedroom bleeding and in a great deal of pain. Let me not also point out that you could make her better with just a small effort. But I guess for you, Aedan the Powerful, that's asking too much. Perhaps I should go and make a few calls. I'm sure that I can have that man come here and take her off your hands so you won't have to have your precious plans fucked up." She hit him again, and this time he felt it cut into his mouth. "That one was for ruining my walk, you selfish overgrown prick."

Aedan laid back down. He was pretty sure that one, if not all, of his brothers was going to be after him as soon as Andi got home. He could hear her crying even now. Looking at the water, he thought of what she'd said to him and hurt for it. Not because of what she said, but because he was afraid that she was right. He was a selfish prick.

~~~

Nikki held tightly onto her temper. She wasn't sure what, at this point, had pissed her off more. The Harrison man who had tried to feel her up, the doctor who was laughing at her right now, or the woman sitting in the chair telling her that she wasn't going anywhere without an escort. Finally having enough, she reached up under the pillow she was laying on and wasn't surprised to find her gun there. Mason had said he'd make sure she had it when he came for her. Pulling it out, she put it on the forehead of the man leaning over her laughing. Surprise, surprise, he stopped laughing immediately.

"I'm not in the best of tempers." He said he could see that. "You're not helping me by laughing at me either. I fucking hurt and I'm confused, not a good combination even on my best days, which isn't all that often. But you're pissing me off more."

"I wasn't laughing at you, but at Aedan." She asked him who that was. "The man's bed that you're currently in. The guy that tried to order you around...your words, not mine. And this is also his house. Do you think you could stop trying to make that weapon a decoration in my head for a moment? I only have one more stitch to put in."

Nikki felt the tears. "I hurt badly. I think that I'm going to be sick too. Do you suppose you could, I don't know, back off for a minute when you're done with that one? I don't want to have to puke on you and tear out the stitches again." He lifted his hands from her body, but she just couldn't stop the pain and gripped harder on the butt of her gun while she breathed though it. Or tried to. "I can't move."

"All right." He—she thought his name was Ennis—didn't move either. "Can Storm help you? She's had some experience with this level of pain." Nikki was vaguely aware of the woman moving toward her. Slowly and with confidence.

"I'm going to touch your arm, all right?" Nikki nodded, but didn't take her eyes off Ennis when Storm spoke to her. "When I do, I'm going to gently lower your arm so that I can take your weapon."

"Don't take it. I mean, you can't take it. I might.... Adkins is out there and coming, you said. I don't want to be without it." Storm said she understood. "All right. But I want you to know that the pain in my chest seems to be connected to my arm right now. I mean, it hurts like a son of a bitch."

As soon as Storm touched her arm, Nikki screamed. She didn't just hurt but was sick with it. When she felt her weapon leave her fingers, she screamed again. The pain nearly took her under. But before she could roll over and throw up, there was a fucking huge tiger standing over her. Whatever had been going on in her belly disappeared right away. And there was the tiger right on the bed, his entire body hard with anger. She had no idea why she knew he was pissed, but everyone in the room backed away.

"It's Aedan," the doctor told her. She started to ask who that was again when she looked at the tiger. "He's protecting you from me."

"What did you plan to do, murder me?" Ennis laughed and the big cat growled. "Oh, shut up. Christ almighty, are you trying to make me hurt more? Get off of me."

Instead of doing what she said, he leaned his massive head down and licked her arm. The pain that she'd been having from the wound there disappeared. Not completely, but enough that she could move without causing her to hurt so badly. Ennis told her to let him see the other wounds.

"Yeah, I don't think so. In the event you don't remember where they are, I'll just let you know I'm not going to let a huge fucking cat get anywhere near my breasts and nipples." He purred. And with his body over hers and so close, she felt it all over her. Looking up at him, she curled her fingers into his mane and pulled his head down so that he was looking at her. His eyes were the same light color as the man who had been under her earlier. The color of the cat, even the darker streaks in his fur, were the same as had been on his head. There was something there, something more, and it occurred to her that Ennis might be right. "Aedan?"

He licked her face. It might have grossed her out under other circumstances, but she tightened her fingers in his fur and held onto him. This was one of the more ridiculous things that had ever happened to her.

"He wants you to let him see the other wounds, please. His saliva can heal you faster than I can with just meds. With these men coming, and we know that they are now, it might benefit you to be healthy rather than banged up the way that you are." She glanced at Storm and noticed that Ennis had left them. "Aedan won't hurt you. He won't be able to. And he'll protect you with his life if it comes to that. Even to the point of you wanting to shoot him yourself."

"That's about where we are now." The cat took hold of

the man's shirt she had on, the one that she'd put on when she arrived here, and tore it off her. "What do you think you're doing?"

He tore at the shirt until it was gone. She lay there, exposed to him, and felt her heart pound in her chest. When he took the first padding in his mouth, she watched him as he gently lifted it from her, but still it hurt. When she cried out, he stopped all movement.

"I had on a vest, but the shooters were really close at the end and it couldn't survive that much pressure." She took the padding in her hand and lifted it the rest of the way off. He moved off her but not the bed. "What do you think is going to happen if you take my blood?"

I already did taste your blood. When I healed the wound on your arm. Nikki stared at him; his voice had come in her head like he was speaking in the room with her. She looked around the bedroom, thinking this whole thing was a joke, and he said her name. *It's me. You know that.*

"You can talk to me." He rubbed his head over her chin and chest, then looked down at her. "Are you going to hurt me?"

No, I can't. I can never harm you or let you be harmed. And I can heal you. Pull the bandages away and let me do it for you. She wasn't sure and said that to him. *You need to be up and about. I just heard from Mason that Otis Adkins took a plane to Ohio.*

"He'll kill whoever gets in his way. I have something, a lot of things actually, that he wants back." He only nodded, didn't ask what it was like most people would have. "It might be better for your family if I left. Grandda...I'm not sure what to do with Grandda. I'll think of something. But if I stay here, someone will get killed."

You're my responsibility now. I have no choice but to make sure that nothing happens to you no matter how much you mess things up for me. It took her a moment, but she thought she got what he was saying. *So if you would please lift the bandages out of the way, I can get this over with.*

Lifting the gun this time wasn't painful. And even if it was, she was pretty sure as angry as she was right now, she might not have felt it. Pushing on his chest where perhaps his black heart was, she pushed the gun into his head so that he would have no doubt that it was there.

"Move." He growled low. "I don't know if you realize this or not, but I think my gun pointed at your head trumps your fucking growl. Now get off the bed, or so help me we will be testing the theory of whether or not I can hurt you."

You're being as unreasonable as I knew you'd be. You think I want this? To have you fucking with my plans after all the work I've put into them? She sat up and barely held onto the moan of pain. *Why are you doing this? Just lay down and let me heal you. Do you want to be killed because you're being stubborn?*

Getting up, she held her gun on him. Reaching for the sheet, she wrapped it around her body and moved to the door. As soon as she found the handle and opened it, he looked ready to pounce. Pissed off now, she fired a bullet at him and it hit less than an inch from his paw. Thankfully he didn't move again, but he did look pissed off.

As soon as she was out of the room, she shut the door and moved down the hall. When a door opened beside her, she aimed at the person there but luckily didn't fire. It was her grandda. And he was armed as well.

"We have to go." He nodded and moved with her. "I don't have a car. Nor clothing. But we can't stay here."

"You kill him?" She said not yet. "All right then. I have both. Money too. We'll be as right as beans and cornbread, see

81

that we ain't."

She hoped so. But she had a feeling that she'd stand a better chance with Adkins than she would with the man upstairs. Adkins might kill her, but Aedan would destroy her.

CHAPTER 6

"I'm guessing you said something to her." Aedan said nothing but sat on his mother's couch and waited. He'd been called home—well, ordered home—an hour ago, and he wasn't any happier about that than he'd been when he saw that old car that had been in his garage for two weeks pulling out of his driveway. "Do you have any idea where she might be?"

"No. I don't even know why she left." Which was a lie. He'd hurt her. He'd seen it in her face when she'd put the gun to his head. "And if you ask me, she's a little too free with trying to blow people's heads off. What if she had shot me?"

"I would imagine that you gave her good reason." His dad, who he thought might understand just a little, had been snapping and biting at him since he showed up. "Did you spout off that crap that you told her grandda? About how she was messing with your time charts or something?"

"I never mentioned charts. But yes, I might have mentioned that she wasn't what I'd had planned for the rest of my life."

He really did feel badly about that. Aedan wasn't normally so crass with his words. To be honest, when he'd felt her pain, it had made him a little on edge. "I could have explained to her what I meant and what I wanted, but she pulled a gun on me and then left. Why was she even armed anyway?"

"I would think that would be obvious, even to you." His mom hit him on the back of the head. "What is wrong with you? Your mate is out there, hurt and being pursued by a man who wants her dead. And not only that, but he's tried to kill her and her grandfather once already. And here you sit whining about how she messed with what you had in the works. I did not raise you to be such a fool, did I?"

Aedan decided he wasn't going to answer that on the grounds that he might get into more trouble. "What would you have me do, Mom? Worry every time something doesn't go her way that she's going to pull a gun on someone? That if we're at some state function that she might have a bad guy come in gunning for her and kill several innocent people?" He stood up. "Her leaving was the best thing that could have—"

The pain took him to the floor. He thought it was his mom, that she'd hurt him, but he knew immediately that it wasn't him that was hurt, it was Nikki. Grabbing the table to pull himself upright, he felt blood on his face and wiped at his nose. His hand came away bloodied.

"What is it, son?"

He couldn't answer his dad to tell him he had no idea. Another pain, this one more powerful, bent him in half. Aedan could hear his mom screaming at him, his dad calling his name. Before he could say anything, darkness swamped him.

When he woke—it couldn't have been more than a few seconds later—he was still laying on the floor. His body no longer hurt, but he stood up cautiously. As he staggered to the door, he knew only that he had to get to Nikki when his Dad was suddenly in front of him.

"She's hurt." His dad nodded. "I have to find her. Something has happened to her and I need to go and bring her home."

"I thought you were just saying how her leaving you was the best thing ever." He turned when his Dad did, and there stood Mason. "I called him. He's going to get her so you don't have to be bothered with her anymore."

"I'm going too." Mason just disappeared. "Dad, where is she? What happened to her? I want to…I don't know what I want, but I need to get to her."

Both his dad and his mom left him standing in the kitchen. Aedan stood there for several seconds before he followed them into the living room. Dad was sitting in his easy chair reading the paper, Mom was knitting something. Neither of them acknowledged that he was even there.

"You're just going to let me believe that you don't give a shit about her." His mom didn't even look up from what she was doing, and told him to watch his language. "My mate is out there, hurt, and you want me to watch my language? What is the matter with you?"

"Nothing. I'd like to tell you that we're lucky that we didn't get to know her better so it won't hurt as badly now that you've kicked her to the curb, but that would be a lie. Because of her grandda. He made her seem as if we knew her as well as he did, and he brought us some of his memories of her that make me think I would have loved her very much." Mom looked at him then, tears in her eyes. "I think you're right, as much as it pains me to say so. You might be better off without her in your life. I know that she certainly will be without you in hers. There is no telling what other cruelty you might have heaped on her."

He sat down. Cruelty? How was that even possible? He'd been honest. With her and with himself. Sort of. Aedan watched his parents as his dad asked his mom what a four letter word was for idiot, and she told him fool. Aedan had no idea why, but he was pretty sure that there wasn't a clue like that in the crossword puzzle that his dad was working on.

When he got up to leave, he didn't bother kissing them good-bye. Neither of them said a word when he told them he was leaving. It was as if he wasn't there, that it mattered little to them that he was hurting by their rejection. He'd not done anything wrong; not so far as he could see, he hadn't. Why were they making him out to be the bad guy in all of this?

Going home, he was met at the door by Winnie. He told him that he'd been cleaning the bedrooms, and asked if he wanted the things that Mr. Neal and Nikki had left behind, that he'd put them in the living room for now. Aedan told him to put them in a box, and that he'd make sure that they got them. When he went into his living room, there was the bundle of things on the table that Winnie had told him about. Aedan picked up the first thing he saw.

It belonged to Paddy, he knew it at first glance. It was his wallet, with nothing in it but pictures. No credit cards or cash. Not that he would have taken either, but Aedan was surprised by their absence. There was a photo album too. The picture on the front was of a child, and he had a feeling it was Nikki.

Leaning back on the couch, he flipped it open to the first page. It was a folded up newspaper article that was yellowed with age. He pulled it out, feeling slightly guilty about what he was doing, but read the headline and decided that he needed to read this. Local Family Gunned Down in Home. He looked at the date and realized that it was Nikki's family.

He read it all the way to the end of the long story. It told how Nikki's father, Nicholas Neal, had been a good cop and a better man. A loving and wonderful father and husband as well. It told how one day Nicholas had walked in on a robbery and had saved two people, the owner and his wife, in a robbery of their store that had gone bad. The would-be robber, a man so high on something that he could barely speak, had tried to kill Nicholas, but only succeeded in wounding the man. The robber was killed when Nicholas, having no choice, had shot the man to save himself.

Then three days after Nicholas had been sent home from the hospital, his wounds barely healed, the family of the robber had broken into his home and murdered him and his wife, Anastasia, as well as shot the couple's only child. It said that she was not expected to survive either.

The townspeople were outraged that something like this could have happened to their hometown hero, and had rallied around the child until her grandparents could come and see to her. The murderers of the family had been put in jail, and there had been no word on what was to happen to them at the time of the article.

Aedan looked at the picture that accompanied the article of the little girl and her family on a beach somewhere. It had been a picture taken during a family vacation, he'd bet. Their faces were full of love and laughter. The date under it with their names was a month prior to the newspaper article. There was another picture in the article, this one of her bloodied body laying between those of her parents. The sheets over them were dark with what he could only assume was blood. Aedan felt his heart ache when he thought of what he'd do if something like that would happen to his own family members.

Aedan moved to the first photo in the album. It was a

newborn baby, chubby and asleep. As he moved through her life, pulling out more newspaper clippings and reading them, he gained a picture of Nikki that he'd doubt very much anyone else would have ever known. Pictures of her and her grandparents on trips. Paddy and her at a shooting range. There were Christmas pictures, birthday parties, and even one of her graduating from high school at the age of fifteen. The article that accompanied that picture said that she had also been taking college classes at night, and would be finishing that part of her education soon as well. It was her dream to be a prosecutor, this article had said.

College had been no different for Nikki. She'd graduated at the top of her class, gone on to get her doctorate in law, then to the police academy. Aedan wasn't really surprised to see that she excelled at that as well. Her grandda was in a picture with her in her blue service uniform.

Nikki had donated her time and money to soup kitchens, and volunteered at shelters when she wasn't working yet another article said. She even read to the elderly at the local nursing home where her grandmother had lived for nearly ten years before her death. The woman, his mate, was someone that he had judged badly and poorly. It was then that he knew that his mother had been right…he'd been beyond cruel to her.

He was reading the last article when he heard someone clear their throat.

"Sir?" Aedan looked up at Winnie. Wiping at the tears on his face, not even realizing that he'd been crying, he asked him what he could do for him. "Browning is here, sir. She'd like a word with you. She is most upset, if you don't mind the warning."

"Tell her to come in."

Aedan didn't put the album back but held it on his lap. He was going to read each article again, look at every picture until he had her memorized. Aedan needed the connection to the small child that had grown up to be a more than beautiful woman. He stood up when Storm came into the room with him. When she slammed her fist into his face, he didn't even fight back. He was pretty sure that he deserved that and more.

"Do you have any idea how fucking pissed I am at you right now? Are all Harrisons...I was going to say men, but I doubt very much you would fit in that category right now. But are you all the dumbest fucking idiots on the face of this fucking earth? You fucking dick weed. I swear to Christ.... Get up. I need to hurt you more." He didn't move and wasn't going to until she calmed down...if she did. "I have my gun. I will shoot you right where you are. I said to get up so I can kick your ass all over this room."

"I'm an idiot." She only crossed her arms over her chest. "I'm not saying that I didn't think this through, because that is just what I did. I thought and thought until I had nothing left to change. And I don't like change. But with Nikki, I was a complete idiot, a fool in the way that I treated her and acted. Like I said, I don't care for changes."

"Well too fucking bad. Because in the event you didn't get it, things get all fucked up and you have to bend a little or I'll fucking break you. You didn't even give her a fucking chance, Aedan. That's not at all like you." He said that he knew that now. "So you want me to believe that you've had this great epiphany and that you've seen the light? Or are you telling me what I want to hear so you won't need to be afraid of me?"

"I don't think there will ever be a time in my life when I'm not afraid of you, Storm." She looked pleased, and he nearly smiled when she glared at him again. "But yes, I guess you could say that is just what happened. I had a look into her life, and I don't care for the way that I assumed she was going to mess up mine. I'm a dick and a jackass. How badly was she hurt this time? And is Paddy all right?"

"There was a car accident about four miles from here. She's in the hospital with some of the stitches that.... How the fuck did you know that?" He told her about the the pain he'd had in the kitchen a bit ago. "Good. Serves you right for kicking her out of your home. I swear to Christ, I could very happily hurt you again right now. I had high hopes for you being the only sane brother in the family. At the very least, the most romantic."

"If I told you that I don't have any idea why I acted the way that I did, are you going to hit me again?" She told him she'd have to think on it and put out her hand to help him up. "Storm, how are they, how is Paddy?"

"Sitting by her bedside, holding her hand like it's the only reason that he's breathing. We're still trying to figure out what happened. There is some speculation that the other driver went left of center. But I'm not buying that shit. And Paddy isn't saying a word. He just sits there looking all of his years." Aedan took her hand then and was lifted up. "You hurt them both, you know that, don't you? When I went to see what I could do, neither of them said a word, but I knew it was you. Then I talked to your parents. You hurt them as well."

"Yes. I know it now. I need to go to see them, but Paddy and Nikki first." He handed her the album. "Read this. And I'm going to change into something nicer. When I get back, will you give me a ride to the hospital? I don't think that I could be safe on the roads right now."

"Yes. But don't be surprised to find your family there and ready to tar your ass up and roll you in broken glass. I might yet help them." He wondered if she knew it was tarred and feathered, but was afraid to ask. Instead he went to his room and pulled on clothing. He had a lot of making up to do, and he was going to start now. When he went back to the living room, Storm looked up from the article she was reading. "I had no idea."

"Yeah, me either. But then I never gave her the chance, now did I?" Aedan pulled on his boots. "I need some favors. I need some security here and at the hospital. And someone to look into this Adkins guy."

"Hospital is secure. The other houses are being watched too. I wasn't sure if I cared if you were hurt or not, so I only have a few watching over here. But I'm upgrading that now. As for the Adkins guy, I have that in a file you can read when we get to the hospital." He thanked her. "What changed your mind?"

He took the album and gave it back to her with the picture of Nikki and her grandda at the end of a pier with a fish between them. They were both smiling, and an air of love seemed to surround them both. Storm asked him why this one.

"That's the day that her grandma passed away. If you read the back of the picture, after making the arrangements to have her funeral, he gathered up his granddaughter and took her out there to help with the pain. He wrote on the back, 'fishing away the pain on this horrific day.'" She pulled it out and read it. Then she looked at him. "My grandda, before he died a long time ago, he told me once that should you ever find yourself in over your head, you should drown some worms. Not fish… he always said drown worms. That's just what they did. Went out there to ease their sorrow and drown worms together. The fish, I would imagine, was an unexpected bonus. Like she is going to be in my life."

"You think it'll be that easy? To bring her around after what you did to her?" He shook his head. "Yeah, I don't think so either. She's hard as nails, and scares me just a little too."

"Say it's not so." She punched him in the arm. "I have to fix this. I'm going to grovel like I've never done before. Beg her to let me try again, and in the meantime, try not to get my head blown off in the process."

"I don't think you're going to be able to make all of that happen." He said nothing, hoping she meant the first things on his list and not the last. He really didn't want to be shot. "I'll help you. A little. But if you fuck up again, you're dead. Not a threat, Aedan, but a promise. I will find someone to kill you and no one will ever know it was me."

He wasn't even thinking she was joking. Aedan doubted very much she knew how to joke around when it came to having people killed. Getting into her car, he nearly told her that he'd walk He'd forgotten what a terrible driver she was.

~~~

Nikki held onto her grandda's hand and said nothing. They were both afraid, she knew. Her especially. Adkins was in town, and he knew for a certainty that they were as well. Adkins had been in the front seat of the car that had come at them, along with the driver, and they had both looked right at them. She was sure that the only reason that they'd gotten out alive was because the airbag had prevented Adkins and his driver from exiting their vehicle before her and Grandda could get away. The old car hadn't any airbags to deflate, so they'd been able to get out and flag down someone to help them right away.

The door opened and she nearly reached for her gun again when she saw who it was. She could not imagine what the fuck he was doing here. But her grandda squeezed her hand and she held tightly onto his. Instead of looking at Aedan, she turned to stare at the blank screen on the television. Anything was better than looking at his handsome face.

"I found this after you left." She didn't turn to look, but her grandda thanked him for it. "I hope you don't mind, but I read it. Most of it. I didn't get to the last one where Nikki had been hurt."

"She was supposed to be dead. You don't know how happy I am that she's not." Grandda let go of her hand and stood up. "If you don't mind, this old man needs a little fresh air. Don't piss her off again, Aedan. I took her gun from her, but she can still put you in a world of hurt all the same."

The door opened and closed and she still stared at the television. She wasn't going to talk to him, and there was no way he was going to touch her. So when he took her hand in his, she jerked it away. He took it back in his, but in a little tighter grip this time.

"I'm sorry." She started to snort, a habit that she was trying in vain to stop doing. "I guess you don't want to hear why I'm such an idiot. I'm pretty sure you have your own list."

"Yes. And I'm not sure why you think coming here right now is going to endear you any better to me. I think you made it perfectly clear that you didn't want me to fuck up your life. Well, jackass, I don't need you to be in mine either. I have things just the way I want them." She looked at him when he kissed the back of her hand. "Don't touch me. I don't want you to ever touch me again."

"Don't you? I was thinking of a few things while I was laying on the floor after Storm hit me. She has a pretty good left, by the way." If he wanted her sympathy, then he was waiting for something that was never happening. "Anyway, I thought of why I didn't want you in my life. For the life of me now, I can't seem to make sense of what I was saying. I'm not even sure why I even thought you'd mess things up for me."

"Well good for you. Now if you don't mind, I'd like for you to get out." He stroked the back of her hand and smiled before he looked at her. Christ, the man was beautiful. But she wasn't going to fall for a pretty face. "Go away."

"I'm glad that you're not armed. What I have to say is going to piss you off again." She asked him why he felt the need to say it then. "Because I want you to understand me. Not me, I guess—that will take a lot longer—but what I was doing by my way of thinking. I was foolish, yes, but I think that it was more than that. I was terrified."

"And that is supposed to mean what to me? I'm afraid every single day of my life. And I'm armed. You're not getting anywhere with me, Aedan. I have to make plans and get out of here before Adkins comes. And he knows that I'm here. I have to make sure that he can't get to me before I can take him down." He ran his finger up her arm to the scar there, and she felt the chip vibrate under her skin. "Don't do that."

"I know what it is. When I tasted your blood, it also gave me an insight to your mind. Your memories and what you were feeling. When you were hurt, I knew it. I just don't know what happened." He stood up and pulled the sheet down that was laying over her. "There was pain here. And here."

The seatbelt had cut into her chest wounds and ripped them open. Also, the buckle had cut into her hip badly enough that she wasn't sure she'd be able to walk without help for the next few days. Her grandda had been lucky; when the car had hit them, it had hit her side or they would never have been able to get out and get some much needed help. Thankfully, they got out of there and to the hospital before Adkins and his men could follow.

When Aedan leaned over her, his eyes watching hers, she held her breath when he kissed the wound over her left breast. Then he ran his tongue over the entire length of it before he moved to the one in the middle of her chest. She stopped him with her hand over his mouth. Her body was on fire and all he was doing was licking her. What would she do if he actually had sex with her? Not that it was going to happen.

"You're not helping yourself if you think getting me all hot and bothered is going to work. I'm made of better stuff. And if I wanted to come, which I'm not saying I do, then I have a vibrator that I can enjoy much more." He grinned at her. "Damn it, don't use that good looking charm on me that I'm sure you've dispatched to hundreds of other women."

"You think I'm good looking? And for the record, women do find me charming, but I've never felt this way about them like I do you." He licked her nipple and she moaned before she could stop it. "I feel that, all the way to my toes."

"Go over there and sit down and tell me what you think you're doing here." He did, but not before he licked the second wound on her chest. This one had been what scared her the most.

Adkins had been so close to her the day of the big shoot out, what she'd begun calling it when she was alone. His gun was only inches from her chest when he fired, his face full of humor and a sadistic laugh. It broke three ribs; she felt each of them as they bent under the immense pressure, then just broke. The second time he shot her from that short distance, she passed out. She looked at Aedan when he sat down, the scraping of the chair bringing her from her nightmarish thoughts. She asked him again what he was doing there.

"I'd like to talk to you. Tell you what is going on in my

head right now. I'm going to be governor. I mean, I'm hoping to be governor here soon. I've been so focused on that, and working at my family's firm, that I sort of lost touch with the world around me. I guess not really lost it, but shut it out. I didn't want to be distracted from.... I wasn't allowing myself to be distracted, when I probably should have a little more." She leaned back. This wasn't really anything she needed to hear, but she thought if he said his piece then he'd go away. It would be safer for him and his family if he did. "I watched my brothers, the two that have mates, change with their love for the women in their lives. Not in a bad way, but in an all-consuming way. Like nothing else mattered but their mates."

"I'm to understand that you didn't want me around because you didn't want to be consumed by me? Bullshit. You just didn't want your well-ordered life to be fucked with. I'm pretty sure that you said that to me too. I don't care, Aedan. You can have your Post-it note, color coordinated socks matching life. I have enough shit in my life to deal with rather than try to remember if I put the damned plastic bottle in the right recycling container." He told her it was the blue one and grinned again. "This isn't funny, you moron. For as much as I hate to admit it, you fucking hurt me. And for that alone, I'm not going to let you come into my life. You...you really hurt me."

"I know I did. And for that I'm profoundly sorry." She looked away, wondering why it mattered that he sounded so sincere. "But I want to tell you what I was thinking. It was a bad decision on my part, I know that now. Like I said, I have been totally focused on my life and didn't let others in. Not even those that matter a great deal to me. I had this all mapped out, and I didn't want love, or being in love, to mess things up. I was stupid in thinking that, when I know for a fact that love does change you, but never the way I was working it out to be. If you ask my mom…well, not today, but if you asked her, she'd tell you that I've always had a sort of one track mind."

"I've tried being on track. But life gets in the way. Everyday things like people trying to gun me down. My parents being shot and killed for simply being good people. My grandma dying too young, when I'd only just gotten to know her a little." He said that he was sorry about her family and that she'd missed so much. But Nikki knew, as surely as she was laying here, that even though he was really sorry, it would never work out for them. And even if it did, there was going to always be someone out there that would take exception to what she did. "Okay, so you've explained yourself. Good for you. Now I think it's time that you left me alone. I have shit to get together."

"Adkins." She nodded. "He's here. I'm sure you know that, but there are nine men with him that we've been able to track down. We think that they're going to try their best to get to you and your grandfather as soon as you try to leave here. People are watching this place very closely to see when they can attack."

"They're in the hospital?" He told her what Storm had told him. "So they're out there, just waiting for me to leave so they can put me in a body bag. What about my grandfather? Is he a target too?"

"I would imagine that they will either get you or use him to get you. It's what Stormy said she'd do. But they'll kill him too, just because he's related to you." She nodded. "I want to help you. My family, we all want to help you. We have a great many resources and people around that can pull together to get you to safety until we can think this through."

"I don't think that you being what you are is going to be

very helpful. I mean, a wealthy businessman who is too big for his britches isn't going to be a blip on his radar. If you know what is on this chip, then you have an understanding of what this monster is and what he's capable of. There isn't enough to convict him, and if we took this to the police, I'm pretty sure that it would either come up missing or we would." He stood up and pulled his shirt off. "What are you doing now?"

"My cat is going to heal you. His saliva is stronger than mine." She watched as he put his hands on the top of his pants and stood there. "Both of us would very much like to eat you too when we're somewhere that we're alone."

Then he was gone. The big cat stood there, staring at her as if she were going to be a fine meal for him, and maybe a little snack later. Thinking of what he'd just said to her, him and his cat eating her, made her squirm a little on the bed.

Nikki wanted to beg him to get out, to leave her to her business. But the thought of his mouth, Aedan's mouth, on her pussy had her soaking wet and her body on fire. The thought of having sex with this man, to have either of them touching her with their mouth, it was all she could do not to beg him for anything he was willing to give her. Then the cat nudged her leg where she'd been hurt and pulled the gauze off with his teeth. Christ, she was so fucked right now.

CHAPTER 7

Aedan knew he had to take it easy with her. He'd fucked up, big time, and he was pretty sure she wasn't going to be very forgiving, at least not quickly. Not that he blamed her. He'd been an asshole as well as an arrogant prick. Both names Storm had called him several times on the way in. But now he had to get her well enough to survive, and maybe mark her as his at the same time. This was a test, he knew, and he was going to pass it or die trying.

Her wounds had been opened again by the accident. He had felt her terror and pain when she'd been hurt, and it wasn't a feeling that he wanted either of them to experience again. Aedan had smelled her blood the moment he'd walked into the room, and had had to work hard to keep his cat calm enough to talk to her. Careful where he put his large paws, he got up on the bed and stood over her. As he watched her, she unsnapped the top of her gown.

"This doesn't change anything. You're just going to help

me out of a bad situation so I can defend myself." He licked her hand. There was nothing wrong with it, but he needed to taste some of her and she was going entirely too slow for his cat. "If you get off the bed, I can stand up and undress. But I'm not going to be naked in front of you. And you can get that whole eating me thing right out of your head."

He got off the bed and watched her stand. She was still wobbly on her feet, but she didn't take any chances with it by not holding onto the bed while she got her feet under her. When she pulled the gown off, Aedan sat on his ass and watched as she started pulling off the bandages. Her hands were trembling, either from weakness or fear, he didn't know which. Distraction; he decided that they both needed a distraction.

Did you know that a tiger's tongue is about twice the length of a human's? She didn't say anything so he continued. *Males weigh anywhere from two hundred to almost seven hundred pounds. We weigh a little more because we're human too. Females are about half that for the most part, but again, as a shifter, they're heavier as well. I think it has to do with muscle mass more than just fat. That's why you will rarely see a fat shifter. And we aren't nocturnal like our counterparts are.*

"Why not?" He was slightly distracted by the sight of her standing there in just her panties and a few bandages. "Aedan, why aren't you nocturnal?"

We're human too, who are not, for the most part, nocturnal. Do you have any idea how beautiful you are right now? She told him to go on with his fun facts. *All right. Our teeth are larger than a human's. Sometimes as long as three inches. Are you going to sit in a chair for me?*

"Are you going to try something funny?" He didn't think what he was going to try could be considered funny, so he

100

shook his big head. "You'd better not. Just heal me so that I can get out of here."

When she made her way to the chair, Aedan talked to his cat. He told him that she was angry with them, mostly him, and that if they hurt her again, broke her heart, they might not ever get another chance to be with her. As he stood up to move toward her, her arousal had him stopping in his tracks.

"What is it?" He didn't say anything but he knew that she was wet. "Just do what you said you were going to do."

Permission, he thought. She'd given them permission to have her. Not really, his heart told him, but his head and cock were all for having it sound like she'd given them the okay. But first, healing her had to happen.

Moving to the chair again, he asked her to pull out the IV needle that had been put there, he supposed, in the event she needed meds. When she took it out, he licked the small wound and watched her face when she looked at it. When she didn't seem to be freaking out, something he was sure she rarely if ever did, he looked at it as well.

It didn't heal immediately, but as they watched it, the wound closed over and there was nothing there to indicate that she'd ever been hurt. The small bruise would take the normal time to heal up. Unless she took his blood into her, she'd not be able to get rid of those just yet.

I told you, the cat's saliva is a lot stronger than mine. And it has this numbing agent in it as well. So when he bites someone, either in play or marking someone, it's not nearly as painful. Nikki, are you all right with this? Just say so and I'll stop and have someone else come in and.... No, I won't be able to let anyone else touch you, but I can stop. She nodded. *All right, love, I'm going to start with the wounds on your chest. Those are the worst, and might need to be taken care of a second time.*

She laid back and he moved between her legs. It wasn't necessary for him to stand there, but it did help him reach her better. Running his tongue over the wound over her left breast, he made sure that his tongue lapped at her nipple that was exposed, too. Her moan had him smiling to himself.

Aedan looked at her before he moved to the next one. She'd been hurt badly, both times by this man. As soon as he could, he was going to find out all he could about this man and make him pay. Aedan was sure if he asked Storm to help him, the man would be gone. It might not be right, but Nikki was his mate and he wanted her to be safe.

When she cleared her throat, he remembered why he was there and licked the next wound, careful not to alarm her too much on how much he was tasting other parts of her. For as much as he wanted her, Nikki trusting him was much more important.

"I heard you tell Grandda that you saw his album. He's been keeping pictures of me since I was taken to him and Grandma." He told her that he'd read about her family being killed. "Yes. I should have died, but for some reason I didn't. I'm glad. I got to be with them for a long time. Grandma had to move into a nursing home after I started living with them. She had a nervous breakdown when her dad died, then later a stroke. Grandda said she and her dad were very close, and when he died, she crawled into her head and never returned. When she died, I felt…I don't know, it was like I was losing more and more of myself every time someone died. I think it's why I make every day count with Grandda. He's all I have in the world. Your tongue is very rough, isn't it?"

Yes. Am I hurting you? She said no and he moved closer to her to touch the wound that had recently been stitched up. Aedan felt his heart break when he saw the other scars there.

Ones that he was sure she'd gotten when her parents had been killed. The only way that they'd leave her body would be if he converted her. Aedan wanted that as much as he did her trust. Trying to think of something else, he licked over the small bump in her arm. *The chip in your arm, you told me that it's dirt on Adkins. Why haven't you used it to bring him in? I'm assuming that you've been working toward that end for a while now.*

"Years, I guess. But as I said, it's enough to bring him in, just enough, but not enough to keep him there. My plan has always been to make a rock solid case against him so that he'd not be out in a few years. And this chip, like the one in Grandda's leg, is what I have so far. But it's here because I wanted to make sure that I never left it behind. I guess in the back of my head I knew that someday I'd have to take off. I just never thought that my grandda would be with me when I did." He licked the small stitched place just below her right breast. This time he didn't hesitate in running his tongue over the rounded flesh, and loved the way her nipple tightened for him. "You're playing unfairly, Aedan. This is not going to happen; whatever is going on in your head right now is not a part of the plan."

Plenty of things are going on in my head right now. Like will your cream be as rich and delicious as I think it will. When you come, will you scream out my name? I'd like that, by the way, to hear you scream my name as I bring you over the edge. Christ, Nikki, I need you. Spread your legs for us. We can smell how aroused you are. She didn't do it at first and he was somewhat disappointed. But when she did move, his cat moved his big head between her thighs and rubbed his nose over her damp panties. *You're so wet, Nikki. Let my cat fuck you with his tongue.*

Her legs widened more for him. And when his cat moved back for her, she removed her panties and slid down on the seat of the chair. Spread out like she was for them, Aedan wanted to take his cat back and have her, but his cat snarled at him that it was his mate as well and he needed her.

Moving close enough to see her hard clit peeking from her swollen lips, it was all Aedan could do not to beg her to touch herself. But his cat moved in and licked her from gate to clit and had her crying out with her first of a great many releases that he was planning to give her.

His cat ate her. Licked her until she cried out twice more before he slid his tongue into her and fucked her that way. When Nikki curled her fingers into his fur and held him, Aedan felt like he'd been given a great gift. Now he had to try not to fuck it up.

Each time she came, he tasted more of her. When his cat backed from her, Aedan looked at the feast before him. She really was beautiful. Especially like she looked right now.

Flushed with sexual pleasure, there was a beautiful dewiness to her skin from what he'd done to her. Her legs were up and over the arms of the chair. Her pussy was wide, wet, and pulsing with need. Nikki's nipples were pink, thick, and hard, and her hands were cupping them as her fingers tugged at the hard nubbins. With her head thrown back and her eyes closed, Aedan wished in that moment that he was artistic and that he could paint her this way.

He took his body back and cupped her ass in his hands and buried his mouth over her pussy. Her scream of another release was like music to his ears, a symphony of sounds that made his cock ache with need.

Words failed him on trying to decide how she tasted. It was more than honey and cream, it was something so unique to her that he knew that for as long as he lived, he'd never get enough of her. Every time she flooded his mouth, when her legs tightened around his head, Aedan knew a pleasure that would keep him warm at night, make him smile when he thought of her. This woman, like none before her, could make him feel like he was king.

Mine, his mind screamed at him; this woman was his and no one would hurt her again. As he devoured her, his fingers sliding in and out of her now, he brought her twice more, her body riding his mouth and fingers like he was taking her. Aedan could not wait to be buried as deeply as he could in her, feel her tighten around his cock, her cream sliding over his balls as he made love to her.

When she lifted his head from her, pulling his hair hard enough that even his cat was startled, he watched her face as she tried to seemingly focus on him. When she licked her lips, all he could think about was feeling her mouth wrapped around his cock while he fucked her there. Aedan moved to her mouth and took it. Kissing her, tasting the dark richness of her mouth, had him pulling her body closer to his, his cock rubbing over her wet heat.

"I need you." He growled low when she lifted his head again. "Christ, do you have any idea how many times that I came? And yet I need more. I need to feel you inside of me, fucking me. Please, I burn with the need to have you inside of me right now, Aedan."

Aedan kissed her again and slid his crown into her pussy. She cried out, her body riding his, but he was careful only to fill her enough to tease them both. For as much as he needed her, he didn't want this to end just yet. Fucking her this way, short strokes in her, she came again. Then she moved in a way that knocked him to the floor.

"You're taking too long." Before he could guess her intent, she moved over him, her hands holding his cock while she slid down his shaft. Aedan couldn't breathe over the feeling of having her there, his body got harder, his cock stretched. When she was seated and started to move, Aedan held her by her hips to still her. "I need to come. Like this, I need to come with your cock inside of me or I'm going to die."

"As do I. But I have to tell you something, I need for you to understand that if I come in you, you belong to me." She nodded, then threw back her head as she rolled over him again. "You're beautiful, Nikki. Come for me. And when you do, you're going to bring me and I want to watch you."

"Watch me. I don't care. But if I don't come with you inside of me, I'm going to be really pissed off." Rolling her to her side, then her back, taking control again, her legs wrapped around his hips and he lifted her up by her ass and fucked her slowly. "You're not helping me."

"Are you always this impatient? Don't you want this to last? I want to have you come on me several times before I fill you." She growled and he laughed. "Christ, to think I was afraid that I'd never get to be this deep inside of you. And now here I am being rushed through what I wanted to last for hours."

"Hours? You can hold on for hours?" He nodded and kissed her before pounding her just a little more. When he lifted his head, he laughed at the expression on her face and fell in love with her. Just like that, Aedan realized he loved his mate. "I might not survive having sex with you often. Oh yes, Aedan. Fuck me like that. Harder, I need to come."

He leaned into her throat and licked the pounding pulse there. She tasted of sex and sweat, a combination that had him sliding into her faster, deeper, and harder. When she cried out that she was coming, he sank his teeth into her throat and nearly came when she dug her nails deep enough into his back to draw blood.

Drinking deeply of her, tasting paradise while he fucked her, he thought of her in his bed, tied to it while he explored her. He had a feeling that was going to be the only way he'd be able to take his time with this woman. And when she cried out again that she was coming, he lifted his head, tilting it, and told her to bite him. Nikki pulled his pec to her mouth and bit his nipple hard enough to have him crying out from the pain/pleasure of it.

He came hard, his body emptying all that he was into her and then filling to take her again. Her body held onto his, her hands touched him everywhere she could reach. And when she came once again, he filled her and he bit her, tearing into her flesh to mark her as his mate. Her mouth over the wound she'd created bonded them in a way that no one would ever be able to break. Aedan threw back his head and roared when she dropped from him.

Rolling to his back when he felt too drained to hold his weight off her, he smiled. Aedan pulled her over him, her warm body spread over his like a comforting blanket. He knew that they couldn't stay here. The door wasn't locked, and he was reasonably sure that anyone within a mile had heard them. Smiling broader, he rolled her to the floor so that he could get up, and looked down at his mate.

Blood was seeping from two of the wounds his cat had not gotten to. Licking them now, he thought about bringing his cat out to help, but knew that they'd still be on this floor if he did that. His cat would want her again, and Aedan was pretty sure she'd had enough for the moment. Reaching for his clothing that he'd discarded before shifting, he pulled on his pants then lifted her to the bed. Covering her with the sheet, he wasn't sure what to do now. His cat snarled at him to take her, but he didn't think that would be a good idea for all the reasons he'd thought of earlier.

There wasn't any way that she could stay here, not with Adkins hanging around and all the innocent people that could be hurt. Storm had pointed out when they got here that the van across the street and the two black cars down from the hospital weren't normal. He hadn't any idea how she knew that, but trusted that she did. So when she'd made a few calls, he asked her what they were to do now.

"Get her healed and home. If you don't, then we're all sitting targets here. And not just the family, but all the people who work here too. Your house, I'm assuming that's where you're taking her, is the safest place for her. You have that fence, the manned gate now, and your house is built like a fortress. Not to say they won't be able to get to you, but with the patrol around your land I'm pretty sure that by the end of any kind of siege they try on you, there will be less of them than when they started out." He had nodded and told her thanks. "I'm going to say this again, Aedan; you fuck this up and I swear to you, you'll never see me coming for your ass."

He believed her. And when Nikki woke up, reaching for what he assumed was her gun, he didn't touch her until she looked at him. Aedan watched her face, looking for some clue as to what she was thinking, but saw nothing. He decided this was another person he'd never play cards with. She was very good at hiding her thoughts from everyone.

"We had sex. A lot of it." He grinned at her and nodded. "Don't be sappy on me, Aedan. I'm not in the mood."

"What are you in the mood for? More? That would be my pleasure, in case you're wondering." She shook her head but he pulled the sheet away. "I could help you. I would love nothing more than to take you this—"

"Aedan? Nikki? I'm sorry, but we have to move now." Aedan looked at Nikki when Riordan pounded on the door to the room and spoke again. "Adkins has left the area; we're going to move you out now while he's gone."

She got out of the bed and stood there. It wasn't until he put his hands on her arms that she looked at him. He could see the confusion there as well as fear, and wanted to tell her it was going to be all right. But he didn't know, and he didn't want to lie to her.

"I don't have anything to wear but bloodied clothing." He handed her his shirt and went to the door while she dressed.

"I need clothing for us both." Riordan said nothing but did look at Nikki. Aedan wasn't sure what was going through his head right then, and was pretty sure that he didn't want to know. For the moment anyway. "She's my mate, and if you say one word about this, I might have Storm hurt you."

"I'll get your bag. But so you know, I'm happy for you both." His dad came down the hall with the duffel from his truck just then and he took it. And the hug that his dad gave him. Just before he entered the room again, Riordan stopped him again and handed him a gun and two extra clips to fit in it. "Tell her it's hot."

Hot. One in the chamber and a full clip in the weapon. When he turned around to hand her the bag, letting her take what she wanted, she was staring at her body. He went to her and held her. She looked a little freaked out.

"You said it would take care of the wounds. I saw that. They're all healed up. I'm freaking out just a little here. My bruising is gone too." He told her because she'd bitten him. "Will...I don't know, will they come back later? After I leave here?"

"You can't leave. I mean you can, but if you do, you'll be

taking me with you. I belong to you now, and where you go, I will too. I can't live without you." She said nothing but pulled away. "Nikki, when we get to my house, we'll talk, okay?"

"Yes. All right. But I'm not blaming you for this. I mean, I nearly raped you." He told her she could anytime she wanted. When she turned and looked at him, his heart broke for her. Aedan waited for her to speak then, afraid of what she might say to him that he wasn't ready to hear. But as soon as she spoke, Aedan knew that they'd be just fine. "I don't want you to be hurt, Aedan. I don't think I could live with myself if anything happened to you and your family."

Pulling her into his arms again, he held her tight. "I don't want you hurt either. And you won't be so long as we work together on this. And you have to see that we need to help you. Christ, I think that Mom would mow him down now if she thought it wouldn't come back and hurt one of us if she did. He's not going to hurt you again so long as I can help it."

They, neither one, said anything more about mating or Adkins. But when they were dressed and headed to the sublevels of the parking garage, he had a feeling that she was going to try and run. To keep them safe. He had to convince her that she wasn't going anywhere.

~~~

Otis wasn't really thrilled with what was going on at the hospital. Yes, there were a lot of armed people around, and they were making no effort to hide the fact. But he'd bet anything that they'd been brought in from the streets, told to stand still, and given a gun, which he'd bet wasn't even loaded. But Joe had told him to wait after pulling the van that they were in around the corner so as not to draw any unwanted attention. So that was what he was doing while Joe went inside to have a good look around and try to get some much needed information. But he was getting antsy and needed to get this done. None of this was making him feel all warm and fuzzy.

When Joe came back to the van, Otis waited while he pulled out his phone and then handed it to him.

"So? This is a very nice picture of the hospital. But in the event you didn't notice, I don't care. Where is Nikki?" Joe took the phone back, made some adjustments, and handed it back to him. He nearly told him that he didn't see it when he did. "Are those military?"

"Yes. There were two at this door until a couple of minutes ago, armed like there is some sort of shit going down that we don't know about, and probably don't want to know either. And the guys out here? More military. They're all over the place in there. Even behind the desk where the computers are." Otis thumbed through some of the other pictures. "I was going to go in there and ask about Nikki being here when this guy stared at me like he not only knew that I worked for you, but what I had for breakfast too. There is some serious shit going on in there. And I hope to Christ that it has nothing to do with us."

So did Otis. But he wasn't sure what else it could have been. He was positive that Nikki knew he was here. They had made eye contact when their cars collided. And so long as he didn't do anything stupid until he was ready, there wasn't any reason for them to arrest him. So far as the regular cops were concerned, he was just a man from another state having a visit. Okay, he did have a dozen or so men with him. And they were more than likely armed with things that would be considered against the law. But that would not get him in trouble so long as he was careful.

"I'm having someone run some plates for me too. A

family, a huge fucking one too—I mean, the size of these men looked like they lifted body builders as a joke—is in there with them. The military as well as the staff. No one says boo to them when they walk around. I saw one of the limos pull up when I was leaving, and watched as one of the men was hugged by an older woman when he got inside. I should know something soon." Almost as soon as he finished speaking, his phone went off. "Harrison. Christ, no wonder. You've seen the name all over the fucking place when we were driving in today, remember? They're considered one of the richest families in the country, and more than likely have ties with the president. The oldest...I have no idea how to pronounce his name. Riordan? Anyway, he's got his fingers in about everything there is. He's married to a woman that is all military herself. Storm Browning Harrison. Another one of them is a doctor, and there is the one I just mentioned that's in politics. I'm thinking that we have just walked in on something that has nothing to do with Nikki, and this place is crawling with these guys over something else. Maybe one of them got a hangnail or they're having major surgery to get the stick out of their asses."

Otis had no idea why, but he doubted that he'd be that fucking lucky. "What floor is she supposed to be on? Where the military is?"

He said he'd not gotten the chance to ask. There were just too many around. Otis watched the men that stood around outside the building from his position. He could see it now. They might have been dressed in suits, but now he could see that they were men at the ready. And if he made a false move, he'd be dead and they'd never bat an eye doing it.

"What could be a single reason this place is overrun by Feds?" Joe said nothing. He wasn't required to answer; Otis was just spit balling out things. "Could it be because of Nikki? If so, why now? Why not when she was undercover working for me and gathering whatever shit that she could? Because I have no doubt that had she been under their care, they would have been all over our asses when we used her as target practice. And that's another thing, why aren't the police or the Feds all over our asses on that? Did she forget who was there with her? Is she withholding information to get me herself? Not likely. I know she's this all or nothing sort of bitch, but she'd not do this on her own if she could get help. Especially after the way we did her the last time."

"You think she has anything to do with this family? The Harrisons, I mean?" He wasn't sure of the connection, but he thought that might be it. "I'm not even sure how to go about finding out without— Mother fuck balls."

He looked in the direction that Joe was. There was Neal. Her grandda was walking with a man that he had no doubt was a Harrison if Joe's description was even close to fact. The guy had to be at least six foot five inches. And he was big too…brawny, his mother would have called him. He figured that if nothing else settled the question of whether Nikki was with the Harrisons or not, this certainly did.

"Do you have an address for any of these fuckers?" Joe said that he didn't but he'd be getting one. "We need to have a little talk with them as soon as possible. See if we can get to Nikki and her grandfather and home with the goods, so to speak, before anyone is the wiser."

"What about the military?" He said he didn't know just yet, but they might not be connected to them. He watched as they walked by the men standing by the front door and weren't acknowledged in any way. "I think, and this is a big speculation on my part, that this is two different things. The

Harrison family and Nikki and whatever these guys are doing here. Let's head to the hotel and see what we can figure out."

"You remember that Robert is there, don't you? He wants to talk to you about joining you in your ventures." Otis nodded. "And I did some checking like you asked. Yes, he is running into some financial difficulties. Seems that his good old dad has a gambling problem, and marrying your daughter just might be the ticket they're looking for to get the house back in order."

He read over the paperwork that Joe had dug up on the Trevino family. The dad didn't just have a problem, but he had a bunch of them. Hookers, gambling, and drugs. The trifecta of fucked up shit. By the time they were pulling up in front of the hotel, he had a better handle on why this kid was taking on his daughter, when for so long, she couldn't even hold a boyfriend for more than a month. Robert was looking for a bank.

"I'm thinking we should make some arrangements to have Dorothea come out here in a couple of days. Tell her that it's a shopping trip or some shit. Savannah too. Might as well show them both what they picked out as the perfect husband in Robert." Joe asked if the pre-nup would hold up. "Yes, but I don't think it will keep him from turning me in if there will be a profit in it. Could be that's why he's trying to get himself working with you to get some good information on me. Holy Christ, that's just what he's thinking. He's going to fucking get some info on me and turn me in. Why else could he be showing this much interest in my business after all this time?"

"I hate to say this, and even though I don't care for the man, I think you're right. And instead of going through all this, I could just kill him. Have it done with and say that he must have skipped town. There won't be a body for them to locate." Otis was tempted, but he told Joe to wait until he talked to Robert himself. "I can do that, but what about the women? You wanna wait, then, to tell them to come out after you and him have a little sit down?"

"Yes, in the event that he gets stupid, or perhaps stupider. That way I won't have to explain to them why he's come up gone. Did the little fucker really think that he could pull this shit on me?" Joe just laughed. "All right. I want to get this dealt with now, so we'll have dinner in the restaurant here in the hotel and talk to him, man to asshole. Then if he isn't going to work out, you can take care of him tomorrow. No body. All right?"

"It'll be like he never existed. What about his dad? You want me to do anything about that shit?" Otis thought about it and said no. "Got it. We'll just let him hang himself out on this one. I think they're pretty close to losing the home anyway."

Otis had seen that too. Fourteen months behind on the house, more than that on the taxes. He wondered how that had been missed when he did the search on the kid at first, and asked Joe about it.

"The house is in his maternal grandmother's name. Didn't know that until I did this search and asked for it. I think that was about the time that he started wanting to be a bigger fish in your ocean. Could be that he figured once you found out, and he knew that you would, he'd want to be so deep in the family that you'd not be able to make him go away. That and that your daughter is in love with him."

"I doubt that Dorothea is in love with anyone but herself. This wedding and all the trimmings is just something to show off with, nothing more. He was just the person who made it happen for her." Joe wisely said nothing. "Let's get this shit going so I can concentrate on Nikki and her death. I need to make sure that she's no longer a problem, and this will just be a minor distraction for us."

As they headed to the hotel, Otis had a feeling that this was only the beginning with Nikki and her grandfather. And that before this was all over, he was going to wish very hard that he'd taken his money and run the first time someone mentioned a wedding.

CHAPTER 8

Grandda watched her like she was a bug on a board with a pin in it. She wasn't sure that she felt any different than that. It was weird not being in so much pain that it took your breath away, living in a house that was as big, if not bigger, than both grandda's house and her own put together, and having more money than she'd ever thought possible because Aedan had put her name on his accounts, as well as the deed to the big house. Walking the length of the room, she thought perhaps it was at the very least one and a half times the size of a couple of semis.

"You're making me crazy. Either sit your butt down and talk to me or go outside and walk. What's the matter with you anyway? You got your bra on backwards?" Nikki just stared at him. "You've been pacing this room like you're trying to wear a furrow in it to plant yourself a garden. Tell me, or so help me I'm tying you to that chair."

"We had sex." As soon as the words left her mouth, she felt her face heat up. "What I mean is, we're bonded, like his

117

people."

"Okay, first, I know you had sex. Christ girl, you look like the canary that had the whole honey pot. Secondly, his people? He's a man for the most part, not some tribe that lives in teepees and rides horses along the fence line." Nikki sat down. "Did he force you? I'm thinking not on account'a him still being up and around and all. And I'm pretty much sure that he's a better man than that. Even if he was giving me some doubts at first. I'm assuming that the two of you worked out his having his life messed up like one of the pasta salads. Right?"

"Yes, I guess we did. And no, he didn't force me into anything. When he said he was going to heal me, things got hot." She glanced at her grandda and he was smiling. "You can't possibly think this is a good thing. We're being chased by a madman and they could all get hurt. And even with the help of their tigers, they can't outwit a bullet. You know this."

"I'm doubting that entered your mind when you were being healed up by him. No more than it did his. And what do you think you can do on your own that you're not going to be able to do with all of them standing behind you?" Grandda snorted. "Most of them have a better gun than I do, and they all know how to use them, thanks to that Stormy. By the way, she's kinda scary, don't you think? Anyhoo, back to guns. Not that they all carry, mind you, but they could, and I'm betting will so long as Adkins is out there."

"They don't have any experience with men like him." Grandda said nothing. "Storm does, I guess, and maybe Riordan. But the rest? They're fancy dressed businessmen who don't have a clue what sort of creeps there are out there."

"You think not? Well, not to hear them talking about it. I've never seen a group more organized in keeping their family safe than these people. That dad of theirs? He's got a good head on his shoulders too. Told me right off that even though I'm ex-cop, that I should really try and listen to his Stormy." Nikki had been told the same thing. "I think you could do a whole lot worse than hooking your horse to this family, Nikki. They don't argue quietly, but they sure do come together when they have to."

"Adkins is going to hurt them. We both know that." Grandda said that he did, but they were better at taking it then he or she might be. "Because of what they are. Yes, they're tigers, but as I said, a bullet can kill them just as quickly as it would a human."

"Yes, it can hurt us. But we can shift and go on while you have to suffer until you get better." Aedan came into the room with them and kissed her on the mouth before sitting down. Too close to her too. When she tried to scoot away from him, he simply picked her up and put her on his lap. Before she could move off him, embarrassed to no end, he rocked upward and she felt his erection. "Now, as I was saying. We can shift and heal from most wounds before you could get to the hospital. Which reminds me, we've confirmed that the van that was outside the hospital was indeed Adkins and his man Joe. The van is parked in front of the local hotel right now and we put a tracker on it. They won't be going anywhere in that thing that we don't know about. Also, there are people working in the hotel that will let us know when something happens."

"Hot damn, I knew you was gonna get this taken care of. See, baby girl, he's already taking care of his woman." Grandda stood up and started walking around. "If I sit for too long, my body just about turns to stone. Anyways, we got nothing on him now. I got me a few friends in the bureau, but that Storm, she said to hold off for a bit. Said she's got herself a whole passel of help that she's got working. Is she really that Browning person? The one that the paper wrote about?"

"She is, and don't talk to her about it. She gets a little touchy sometimes because people only remember that about her. Not her delicate ways or her softly spoken words." All three of them laughed and Aedan hugged her to him as he continued. "Storm has some people in high places that she's working with. And Howard let her know that you two are related to him."

"He's my son. Don't let that get around much either. Hard to be undercover when you're popping up in the news all the time." He started pacing again but slower, careful of where he placed each foot. That was when Nikki realized that no one had healed him. "Adkins is going to be desperate now that he knows where we are and that we've gotten all the wagons in a circle. Thinking he might be taking his time for the moment, but he won't for long."

"Why would he do that now that he knows that you're both here? Wouldn't he just, I don't know, come after you quickly to finish this and get out of town?" Nikki wasn't sure how to answer that for Aedan. There was plenty that would piss Adkins off if he found out just a part of what she had on him. But Riordan and the rest of the family came into the room, and the ones that she'd not met already were introduced to her and Grandda.

"You asked a good question there, Aedan, and if you don't mind, I'd like to share with you what my Nikki and I have on him." He nodded at her and she told him to continue. The Harrisons needed to know everything they were dealing with. "Adkins and I tangled up before. Mostly it was his informants at the station house, but he had a few others in his pockets too. Some of them deeper than others, but for the most part, there were not that many government people around that didn't have some sorta in with Adkins and his crew."

"You mean that he was paying them off or blackmailing them." Paddy told Storm that it was a little of both, but mostly just paying them. "Yeah, no different than in my line of business. Some people are just too fucking greedy for their own good."

"You got that in one. But this here feller, he decided that being sixth in line for the king job in the city wasn't enough, and he started making headway into taking a little more. Nikki and I have been gathering what we could for the last few years. And it's all on a drive we got put in us." Grandda sat down and pulled up his pant leg. She showed them her arm. "There isn't enough to convict yet, close but no cigar. He'd be out in no time, and no less like a wet hen for it. Plus, we'd have to be careful who got this stuff. We have to keep it from falling into the wrong hands. Most of this was gotten by Nikki when she was undercover."

"And he found out." Grandda told Riordan they weren't sure how that come to light. "I do. The partner that Nikki had, the handler. He was starting to be blamed for the amount of shipments that were being intercepted by the Feds. So he tagged you. Wasn't sure myself what that meant until Storm told me. But he got just enough information to go to Adkins and turn you in. That was just a few weeks before you were shot."

"There were four of them, men that were following your every move and reporting it back to him. Once he had that you were making some calls to someone — lucky for you they never figured out it was your grandfather — they knew that you were the mole. Or assumed you were. You were too tricky for this handler, so when he turned you in, you were blamed for other things as well. Most of them were to cover shit that he'd been doing. Two days before the shooting, he went to Adkins and struck up a deal." Nikki asked Storm how she knew this. "Your handler wrote out a long, very detailed accounting of every meeting he had with Adkins, as well as a few recordings he had, and put them in a safety deposit box that was to be opened if he came up missing. They were found after his body was. Apparently when you disappeared, Adkins took his temper out on this guy."

She started thinking, her mind going in several directions at once. Looking at Aedan, she let her mind settle, focus on something else besides what was going on in her head. It would come to her, whatever was there, but she had to wait for it to find her.

When you look at me like that, all I can think about is having you spread out on our bed naked. Her body warmed up, and her nipples hardened in her bra. When he growled at her, the sound of it like a caress on her skin, she nearly reached for him when someone laughed. *Perhaps we should think of something else.* Then it hit her.

"Adkins future son-in-law, Robert Trevino, is in debt. To his ears about now." When they stared at her as if they had no idea what she was talking about, she looked at Storm. "He'd be able to shed some light on movements. Let us know when Adkins returns home. How many people he sees around the property. That way we can keep an eye on the household, see when they start to scatter. It'll tell us when he's ready to act."

"I have people at his home, in it too. But you're right, the closer we have someone to him, the better. Problem is, Trevino isn't in house. Not for the last few days. And according to the intel we're getting, the household is in a tizzy about something." Nikki said it was the wedding. "Okay, that makes sense. The wife and daughter, they've been going to bakery after bakery, as well as a few catering services. We'll get some people around for that too."

"He'd be here." She asked her grandda why he thought that. "That's where I'd have my future son-in-law should he be joining the family. Get him right in the thick of things so if he does the nasty to someone other than my daughter, he'd have firsthand knowledge of what might happen to him if he's caught with his pants around his ankles and the woman he's banging ain't my precious."

Storm laughed. "You know, I like you, Paddy. You have a way with words that makes me think you might have been a blast to be around when you were a Fed. Don't have a lot of use for them for the most part. Dressed up dolls most of them, but you might have been fun." Grandda told her he'd been able to shake a few nuts out of the garden before. "Yes, sir. I do think I'll enjoy working with you."

So in the end it was decided to see where Trevino might be. And if he was here, they may or may not be able to use him, but it was something they could fall back on. When dinner was called they all joined together in the dining room, but she noticed that no one spoke of anything but family and what was going on outside of this crisis. She looked at her grandda, who most of the time would help her with a case well into breakfast the next morning when she needed. With his wink, she looked at Aedan. This was what a family, a normal family, was like, she supposed.

~~~

Nikki was nervous. So was he, but he was used to the house, she wasn't. As she made her way around the room again, he sat down on the chair that had been in the house when he'd bought it. The bedroom suite had been his in his old place,

123

but he loved this chair and had kept it in here. Waiting for her to speak, he thought of the things that had been discussed tonight and what plans had been made to keep everyone safe.

"I'm guessing that you were born with a silver spoon in your mouth and spit it out when it wasn't gold." He wasn't sure why she sounded angry, but told her that yes, he'd been born with money. "I don't have any. I mean, there was some in a savings account, but I think we've run though that while we've been on the run. Grandda also has money in that old beater of his, but that is running money."

"You don't have to worry about money if that's what you mean." She said nothing, but picked up a framed picture of his family taken at Riordan's wedding. "I work hard. I'm a partner in the family business that goes to companies that are struggling and tells them how to get things back under control. Sometimes that means telling them that there's no hope, but we exhaust every other avenue before we get that far."

"Do you buy them up, make them work for you, and fuck the others working there?" The anger was nearly palpable this time. "Like those men who buy up orphanages and toss everyone out on the streets?"

"No, usually we make the youngest work for us, putting the bullets together that we use to kill off the ones that are no longer any use to us." She turned and looked at him. "No, we don't buy companies, nor orphanages, and make them work for us. Would you mind telling me why you're so hostile to me?"

"I don't know." She set the picture down and moved to the dresser that he'd cleaned out for her. "I don't have any idea how to be a person you would want to date, much less be around. I can't stand fake people, not that your family is, but you would be hanging around with ones that are. Especially since you have aspirations of becoming the next governor."

"I also am thinking about pursuing the White House. Would that bother you so much?" She only shrugged at him. "Are you pissed off at me for some reason? Or does the fact that I have money piss you off?"

"How much do you have?" He told her. When she nearly dropped the vase in her hand, he stood up. "You have a billion dollars. Right now, you could call someone up and say I need you to buy me a mansion, and you'd not have to finance it."

"I would though. It's better financial sense to finance some things. A house is one of them. I'd buy low, sell high if that was in the plans. But right now, I love this house and where it is in proximity to my family." He touched his hands to her arms and held her until she looked at him. "However, if you don't care for this house, or think that it's not anything you can grow old in with me, we can certainly find something else."

"Why would you do that when you obviously love this house?" He told her because he loved her more. "No, that's not possible. You just like the sex. I do as well, but there is no reason for you to say those sorts of things to me."

"I'm not going to ever lie to you. Not that I could, but I'd not even if there wasn't this sort of DNA thing that prevents it." He watched her face as she digested that. "You're not giving me a chance at all, are you?"

"I don't know what you're talking about. I'm just thinking about what you said. You have to love me because you've been made that way. You think to impress me by telling me that we can sell this beautiful house if I don't like it, and on top of that, you want me to be something and someone I'm not so you can run for office." He felt his own temper rise up. He pushed her onto the bed and started to take off his shirt.

"So now we're going to have sex because you're pissed off."

"No, I'm going on a run. And while I'm out, trying my best to think of why you're so angry, I'm going to have my brother find a realtor and put this house on the market. As for you changing for me? I never once asked you to do that, nor did I, if you recall, ever say to you that you had to."

He let his cat take him when he was naked. But before he could go out the side door that had been opened when they came here tonight, she stepped in front of him and stopped him.

"I don't know what I'm doing." Aedan said nothing. "I mean, I have no idea what the fuck I'm supposed to do with a nice man who has money to burn and cares enough about me to sell his home to make me happy. No one has ever done that for me...or for anyone I know before. And instead of hitting me, like I think I thought you would so I'd have an excuse to be even more pissed at you, you walk away."

Aedan sat down and waited for the rest of it. Because as surely as he was sitting there, he knew there was more. Instead of talking though, she moved out onto the deck that was his favorite part of this room. When he joined her as his cat, he leaned against her leg and was glad when she put her fingers in his fur.

"I'm a basket case of worry right now. I know that you and your family will do whatever it takes to keep my grandda and I safe, but who will take care of you?" She sat down so that they were eye level now. "I'm scared out of my mind. More so than when I was told to drop to my knees on that street, knowing that I was as good as dead."

Aedan pulled his cat back and lifted her onto his lap. She didn't struggle to get away, but leaned on his chest while he held her. He thought of all the things he could say to her, and decided that he'd just be honest with her.

"When I found out you were my mate, all I could think about was how this was going to take time from the plan that I had. I've always been someone who likes to plan. Business and my personal life. Going on a date was no different." He laughed a little. "I'd pick the woman up, who would never be ready on time, take her to the restaurant where I had made reservations, and order for us both. The women I dated before you, they would expect that. For me to take control and to make sure that they were pampered and well cared for. Sex with them was no different. It was cold, I know that now. They enjoyed themselves, I made sure of that, but it wasn't fulfilling to me. Because, as you might have guessed, I was planning the next move. Mostly to break it off before they got in the way."

"And do you do that when you have sex with me?" He told her that he made love with her, and no, he didn't. "Then what is it you think about? What you need from the grocery store? How to get me to stop telling you what to do?"

"No. I think of nothing but making you scream out your pleasure. The need to know how you taste on different parts of your body is first and forefront in my head." He turned her on his lap and leaned back against the wall behind him as she straddled him. "I wonder how you'd feel about being tied to my bed while I took my time with you. What you would do if I asked you to run naked in the woods beyond here and let my cat eat you again."

"I love the feel of his tongue in my pussy. You were right about that; he does have a very long tongue." Aedan licked her throat and then pulled her blouse up and over her head. Taking her bra up over her breast, he suckled at it until she began to ride him in quick strokes. "I could come this way, with my clothing on and you only sucking at my breast."

"I'd love to run you down as my cat. Take you against the closest tree while you scream out that you're coming for me." He grabbed her hips, and her pants came off in shreds. "Ride me, Nikki. Come on my cock so that I can taste you while you enjoy this."

He helped her slide over him, and when she was seated, her pussy wrapped around him so tightly that it bordered on painful, he kissed her. Showed her with his mouth how much he truly did love her.

Her ride was erotic and slow. As much as he wanted to hurry her, feel her tighten around him more in pleasure, Aedan watched her face. She was beautiful when she was close, her face tight with need, her mouth open only a little so that she would pant for him. And her breasts pinked up. Her nipples that were a dusty rose would pucker as well, seemingly begging to be bitten. When he took one into his mouth and suckled on just the tip, Nikki held him to her, riding his cock faster.

Cupping her ass, he brought her to his body with each downward stroke. He knew that she was enjoying this, the hitch in her breath telling him that she was close to coming. And when he bit down on her nipple hard enough to draw blood, she threw back her head and screamed. Aedan watched her face as she came three more times.

"Come with me." He wasn't ready to end this and told her so. "Please, you'll bring me again, harder when you come in me. It's like your cum is a flame that fires off a rocket inside of me. Please, Aedan, set me off."

He rolled her to the floor and her legs wrapped around him. Fucking her now, pounding her as hard as he could, he could feel her holding him within her, her hands dug deeply into his muscles. And when she tilted her head, offering up her throat to him, Aedan didn't hesitate but leaned into her and snapped his powerful jaws into her skin, and he emptied himself into her. He tasted the difference immediately…this was a deep bite. Too deep.

He hurt her. When she screamed a second time, he lifted his head and blood sprayed him in the face. She was going to die if he didn't do something, and he leaned to her wound and started to seal it when she told him to finish her. It took his addled mind a second to realize what she meant.

"Now, change me. I'm close." He told her that he couldn't do that. Not without her trust. "You bit me hard enough to kill me and I'm asking for more. I don't think I could trust you any more than that."

Aedan knew she was right and his cat took him. When he licked the wound at her throat closed, he could hear her slowing heartrate. Moving to her belly, he tore into the part of her just above her naval, and cringed when she cried out again. Tearing into her skin, biting through her bowel, Aedan prayed he didn't kill her when he moved to her leg.

This time she made not a single sound when he bit her. She was unconscious by now, her body shutting down in an effort to try and save itself. When his cat was satisfied that he'd done what he could, Aedan took his body back and laid beside her while he waited for something, anything to tell him that he'd not just killed the only woman that he'd ever love.

"When this is done, we're getting married. And you're going to say yes. I can't stand the fact that you're not my wife and now you might be dying on me." He kissed her gently on the mouth and licked the wound that she'd made there with her teeth. "You knew what you were doing, didn't you? Did Storm put you up to this? If so, you can bet we're going to have a little talk when you're better. Please get better, Nikki.

I need you."

When she shivered a little, he got up and placed her on the bed and covered her so that she'd not catch a chill, then sat down to watch her. Aedan was ready to call his brother, Ennis, in when she opened her eyes and looked at him.

"I feel her." That's all she said to him before she closed her eyes and smiled. Aedan could hear it then. Her heartbeat was getting stronger and her skin was no longer that deathly pale color. Christ, he'd just turned his mate into a tiger without asking anyone if he should or not.

CHAPTER 9

Otis looked at the man in front of him. He'd been beaten to shit, and up until twenty minutes ago, he had still maintained that he'd had nothing to do with the wire on his chest when they'd sat down to dinner last evening. Joe stood behind Robert, nursing his knuckles for either the next round or to use the gun that was laying on the small table in front of him. Robert had been a hard nut to crack.

"So you're no longer telling me that this wire just appeared taped to your chest, and that perhaps you might have gotten it from the shirt you had on? That instead, you got it to entrap me into telling you shit that you could use against me? Is that about right?" Robert's head lolled to the side, but he nodded then shook his head when Otis asked him again. "You're either pretty stupid or you think I am if you want me to believe that you thought of this on your own. You fucking moron, you were sent here by the Feds. What did they promise you? That your family home would be out from under the staggering debt that your daddy dearest put you in?"

"No Feds, I promise." He was beginning to believe that too. But someone had wired him up. And for the sole purpose of getting shit on him. "Dad. He said that we'd use it to get out of the pre-nup. But I had my own plans. That paper you had me sign? It wasn't going to mean shit to me when I was done."

Now they were getting to the heart of things. With a short nod to Joe, he waited until he was gone to speak to Robert again. Joe would make sure that Robert senior would pay for this shit. He wondered if Robert had ever loved his daughter or if he had had these plans for her after they were wed all along. It mattered little now…Robert was as good as dead.

"My daughter. She have anything to do with this? Did she know what you were about?" He shook his head and said Sandy. "My wife, Savannah? You call her Sandy?"

"Fucking her." Otis let that roll around in his head for a moment. His wife was fucking around on him? With his future son-in-law? For fuck sake, this was bad. "Didn't like that she was held by the same paperwork. We became lovers before I met your daughter."

"So the two of you figured you'd fuck me and my daughter and come out on the other side of the pre-nups by what, killing the two of us off? Is that right?" Robert said that was their plan, but not his dad's. "He didn't know about the other, that you were screwing my wife and had your own little way of dealing with me?"

"No. He figured with a little of the right information, he could go to the Feds, like you said, and get you out of my life and be paid a little extra while he was at it." Robert laughed. "I'm guessing that even though I'm telling you the truth, you're not going to just let me go, are you?"

"Hardly. Did my wife know about the wire? Or was that just you and good old Dad's little plan?" He said she knew it all. It was the reason he'd been told to come here. "I see. And what did she plan to have happen to you when I found out? Because the two of you together, you don't have enough brains to have pulled this shit off."

"You think? Well, I did get you to spend all that money on a wedding that wasn't going to last longer than it took for me to take her on our honeymoon. Tragic things happen when you're in a different country. Didn't you know that?" He was baiting him, Otis knew it. But he wasn't finished with him just yet. "You might want to check on some of the vendors *Sandy* was using too. You might find that they've never heard of a wedding between the Trevinos and Adkinses. She is one smart cookie, your little wifey. We were going to be rich as fuck, living and laughing about how we'd taken down the great Otis Adkins."

He'd been had. Not just a few times, but a great deal it appeared. Otis had a thought that perhaps that was where the information from his lost shipments had been going to, but didn't ask. He wasn't sure he could have taken much more right now. But he had to deal with this shit before anything else.

"You do know that you and my wife, you're not going to ever be found, don't you?" Robert only grinned. "And I would imagine that right about now, your entire family is sitting on their knees waiting for the bullet that will end their association with this world." Robert looked at him, his face now full of fear. "What? You really didn't think this was going to end with your father and you, did you? I'm a man that prides myself on not leaving witnesses. And as surely as you're telling me this, you can bet your momma knew too. You should have just been happy to marry my daughter and reaped the benefits from that. Not think you could take a man like me."

"My sister didn't have anything to do with this. I'll make you a deal, tell you where the money is. Just don't kill her. She's doesn't know shit." Otis smiled. "You can't kill her, you fucking bastard, she's just a kid. I've given you everything you need to take the rest of us down. Leave her alone."

"She might have lived a little longer had she not been related to you." Robert started screaming then, and his first attempt at begging came when bartering did him no good. Otis had to get out of here, had to think. Going to the table where the gun was laying, he picked it up and put it to the back of Robert's head. "Tell your father I said to go fuck himself."

Firing once was all it took to end the man's life. But Otis shot him four more times just because he could. When Joe came back a few minutes later, saying that the rest was taken care of, Otis told him to call his wife here. There was going to be a reckoning today, and everyone was going to know that he was pissed off.

"Also, I'm tired of fucking around with Nikki. Get me someone here that will bring her to heel. I don't care who it is or how badly you have to knock them around, so long as they're alive when she gets here."

Going back to his hotel, he made a list of all the places he could remember that Savannah had taken him to. Most of them had stupid names, easy to look up once he thought about what they'd be supplying to him and this wedding. By the time he'd arrived in his room, Otis had a pretty good start on the list. The first business he called was the fucking bakery that had screwed up the flowers.

"Trevino? No, I don't think we're doing that wedding. Let me check." When he was put on hold, Otis looked at the list of other businesses. Yes, he was pretty sure that he had—

"Here it is. Yes, we did have a seating for that name, but no one showed to do the taste testing. It is very important to our company to make sure that there are no surprises at the wedding, when it is too — "

Otis hung up. It was enough, he realized then, just to have been fucked over once. Joe would have her here within a few hours, and then he'd take care of her as well. This fucking shit was going to be the last time he ever had to deal with things other than business. He might even bring his daughter in. He was sure that once she found out about her mother and ex-fiancé's betrayal, she'd be on board with about anything. Keeping it in the family.

When he heard from his wife, he told her that he really missed his girls. Then he made arrangements to have her go on a little spree just for her. By the time they had it all set up, Otis was exhausted. Savannah was on her way out, and she had a list of things that needed a deposit on them as well when she got here.

"This wedding is going to be epic, Otis. You wait and see. And our little girl is going to be happily married to a better man than we could have ever hoped for. I do hope that he is working out with you. You taking him on this trip, it might be the best thing for the two of you." He told her that he'd spent the evening and well into the morning with him. "Well that's perfect. Don't you think? The boy just loves Dorothea, and I'm happy they'll be married to spend the rest of their lives together."

"You have no idea how much I've enjoyed having him here either. We've done so much together." She gushed about how happy she was, and finally he had to get off the phone with her or scream at her that he'd enjoyed killing her lover. "I have to go, love. Joe is here and he has some updates on things for me."

"You go. But remember, I'm going to need you to give me some cash when I leave. These vendors nowadays, always wanting cash. Do you suppose they don't report all their earnings to the IRS and pocket this?" He told her someone was certainly pocketing it. "What?"

"Never mind. I'm just exhausted. Once you get here, I'll be able to relax again. We'll have an evening of it, you and I." She told him she'd need a new dress for that. "You go right ahead and buy whatever you need. Just come here so we can celebrate."

He looked at Joe, who had been seated at the table with him, when he got off the phone. Joe said nothing, didn't need to. When Otis got up and poured them both a drink, he asked him about the Trevinos.

"They'll be found in the morning, I would guess. It looked like they were headed out of town. Don't know if there was some kind of code from Robert on when they should leave, but I think something triggered it." Otis said it was more than likely the wire going down. "Could be. What do you want to do about Savannah? I'm assuming that you want her to run into some trouble on the way here, and that's why you sent her on this shopping spree alone. It's no problem for me either way. I'm going to enjoy this regardless."

"While she's out and about. I thought I wanted to talk to her, see her face when I told her that her lover was gone, but I need to complete this shit with Nikki. It's costing me." Joe said he'd take care of it. "Just make sure that she knows what we know, all right? I don't want her thinking, even in the afterlife, that she might have pulled the wool over my eyes."

"I'll take care of it. Also, I'm going to pick someone up for you tonight. I have an eye on just the right person." He nodded. "Where do you want me to take them?"

"Whoever it is might as well know that we mean business. Take them where poor Robert is laying." He nodded and stood up. "When this is done, we're going to leave the country for a while. Have things ready."

"I will. Taking Dorothea too?" He said that he was. "Good. I'll make arrangements for that as soon as I deal with Savannah. I have to tell you, Otis, I didn't see that one coming. I'm sorry about that."

"I didn't either. None of it. But better now than after the wedding. Christ, I've never been so taken in all my life. And by my own wife." Joe only nodded. "But now I can take care of Nikki and not have to worry about anything else. And once she is gone and forgotten, we can concentrate on what matters, making some money."

~~~

"I've been thinking about some of the things you brought up at the debate the other night. And if you'd be so kind as to have a meeting with me, without the press, I'd like to go over them. I mean, the reason that I've not dealt with them as yet." Aedan looked at the speech he'd been working on for the women's tea tomorrow afternoon when the phone had rung. His mom had asked him to do it, and he couldn't turn her down. "Say we meet for lunch today. At my place."

"I have a lot going on right now, Dewey. How about you and I meet for dinner? My wife and I were going to be trying that new restaurant in town, and you and your lovely wife can join us." There was no way he was meeting this man in a private setting. He might be new to the political game, but he wasn't stupid. "My dad and mom said it's really good, and I'm trying to help out a new local business."

"Sure, sure. I guess that would be all right. You give me

the address and I can have it checked out for me. Can't be too careful when you're the governor of a fine state like Ohio, now can you? But dinner might be cutting it too close for my men." A paper slid in front of him and he looked up at Nikki, who had been helping him with his speech. The note simply said *bugs/cameras.* He frowned. But before he could ask her what she meant, Dewey started talking again. "I had no idea you were married. I thought.... Well, I think everyone thought that you were off the market for that sort of thing. Don't you have a bevy of women all over the state?"

The laughter was forced. And while he was trying to think what to say to him, another note appeared. *He wants to bug the place and put in cameras so that he can have dirt on you.* He looked at Nikki and she shrugged. Really?

"I'm sorry, but if you can't make tonight's plans, I won't be able to see you until after the second rounds of debates, I'm afraid, what with Thanksgiving next week then Christmas right around the corner. Well, you know how demanding family can be. Not that I'd change a thing about them. So what do you think?" Nikki nodded at him and leaned back in her chair. "It might be January before I can get with you if not."

In the end Dewey said he'd be there, but to make it seven instead of six. When he agreed then hung up, he asked Nikki why she thought that. She got up to pace while she spoke.

"I'm going nuts here, just so you know. Anyway, why is he doing this? Because you have no skeletons in your closet but for the fact that you're a cat. You don't need to take bribes because, let's face it, you have all the money. The only way he's going to be able to make you look bad is to make you lose control of your animal where people can see you. Barring that, where he can record it happening. Or he takes recordings of you speaking, then manipulates it into something that you'd never in a million years say but he's got it on tape." He asked her why she was bored. "Because I'm used to working my ass off all the time, and when not working, I had shit I was looking into to work on. This place is perfect, not that I'd have any idea how to make a house beautiful, and if one more person asks me how it feels to be a cat, I might show them how monstrous they can be."

"Come here, love." She said that she didn't want him to cuddle her. "I want you to cuddle me."

"You're a jackass." He laughed and patted his lap. "We're not getting anything done but having sex. You know that, right?"

"I thought you enjoyed that about me." She just glared at him. "Have I told you how beautiful your cat is? Who would have thought you'd be white?"

"I can't do anything by half measures." He laughed again. "I had so much fun last night when I woke up. Christ, that is the most freeing feeling, being able to leap over things and roll with falls like I've never been able to before. But the sex.... Well, to be honest, it was sort of a letdown. With the cat anyway."

"I told you it would be. But I think I more than made up for it after he finished with your cat." She nodded, and he could smell her body ready itself for him. "Come here, love. I'd very much like to take you right here on my desk."

She came to him then, her body moving like she had been a cat her entire life. And when she was in front of him, her blouse opened all the way to her naval, pants undone, Aedan pulled her close enough to taste the skin she'd exposed for him.

"I love the way you make me feel. Pretty and sexy." He told her that she was. "Not really. But you do make me feel that way."

He pulled her pants off while she took her blouse off for him. When she stood before him in only her bra and panties, he sat her on the desk and put her feet on his legs. When she leaned back, it was all he could do not to stand and take her right then.

"I'm going to eat you until I've had enough. Might be a while, so I hope you don't mind." She shook her head at him. "Eating you last night, while you were leaning against the tree, will be a memory that I never forget. Not for as long as I live."

"Hurry. I'm so needy." He pulled her panties aside and licked her. "Yes, more. I want to feel your tongue inside of me."

He did as she asked and was rewarded with copious amounts of her cream when she came for him. As he devoured her, ate her ravenously, he fucked her with his fingers and felt more of her cream run down his hand.

There was something so exciting about her spread out before him this way. She was hot and ready, and knowing that she was his and his only made him feel like the king of the world. When her fingers curled into his hair and she pulled him closer, Aedan reached down and undid his pants to free his cock.

He needed to take her, mark her as he'd done last night. Christ, she'd bitten him in the thigh, and it had nearly taken his head off when he'd come. Then when she was Nikki again, he'd fucked her so hard that he had nearly passed out when he'd come with her.

"Fuck me, Aedan." Standing up now, he slid his cock over her clit, watching her face as she cried out several times that she needed more. So when he slammed into her, his cock buried to the hilt, he paused for a moment, just enough that he could catch his breath. But she wasn't having any of it.

With her legs wrapped around his hips, she pulled him down to her and he kissed her. As soon as she rose up to meet each of his downward strokes, he knew that the end was coming up fast. His balls ached so badly that he was sure he was going to be sore in a little while. But when she pulled his throat to her mouth, Aedan closed his eyes for what he knew was going to be a killer climax.

Her teeth grazed his skin, teasing him. When her tongue brushed over his pulse, he held her to him, cupped her ass, and brought her as close as he could. The moment that she bit him, not only did Aedan see stars, but he was pretty sure that there were fireworks, birds, hammers, as well as a few other sparkling items that he simply could not name. He came so hard that he was sure that he'd never be able to repeat it again.

As she cried out that she was coming, Aedan looked into her eyes. He wanted to see her, look deeply into her when she released. As soon as she came, her body nearly bowing up enough to unseat him, Aedan saw her cat there.

She was standing on her hind legs, her paws up, and she looked magnificent. Her white fur was standing on end, the dark stripes of their kind darker because of the lack of any other color. And when she dropped to her paws and roared, Aedan felt like he'd been given a rare gift in his mate, one that he'd protect with his life.

"I love you." He held her as her words, softly spoken, entered his heart. "I love you so much that I ache with it, Aedan."

"I love you as well. And will forever and beyond." He held her to him, his body so relaxed that he marveled that he could still stand. "I'm looking forward to spending the rest of my life with you at my side."

When they were rested enough to move, him barely, they dressed. Sitting in his chair again, he held her in his arms. Nothing felt this good, he was sure. And when she snuggled up under his chin, he had to smile. Two weeks ago had someone said she'd want to snuggle, he would have laughed. He was pretty sure she might have shot the person.

After a short knock, the door burst open. He wasn't sure what was going on, and nearly shifted until he saw his new butler. Winnie came into the room with the strangest look on his face. It was a combination of terror and being ill. Aedan drew his gun, and he noticed in a vague sort of way that Nikki had as well. Whatever was going to happen, they were going to be as prepared as they could be.

"Your brother.... Riordan is in the kitchen on the.... They called here when they couldn't get to.... I didn't know if I was to call you, but...." Nikki went to the tall man and slapped him on the cheek. He looked at her for several seconds before he thanked her. "My mouth was frozen, sir. But your father, Mr. Harrison, he's been taken."

"Taken? When?" He told him what he knew. "Christ. It has to be Adkins. Have the police been called? Does the rest of the family know?"

"Yes, sir, they're on their way here as well. And Browning has asked that you don't go off halfcocked. She said that she wanted to talk to us before we did anything...well, sir, she said before we did anything fucking dumb before she got here."

Aedan knew as surely as he was standing there that someone was going to be dead by nightfall.

CHAPTER 10

Ordan didn't lift his head when he woke up. He'd been around enough to know that you got your bearings before you let anyone know you were aware. His head hurt worse than anything he'd ever felt before, but he knew that being alive right now was better than the alternative. He reached out and found his lovely mate upset, and told her he was all right.

You old fool. What are you doing being kidnapped like some teenager on a whim? He told her he was powerfully sorry about that. *You have me worried sick, and the boys are beside themselves. Stormy is ready to come there and kick your bottom for making me.... Are you all right?*

Yes, I am, love. Head hurts like it did that time I walked into a beam in the basement when the lights were off. Should have known better than to think I was gonna be able to see in the dark. He was babbling, but it was better than thinking about what had happened. *You tell them boys not to get themselves hurt over this. I'm doing just fine and dandy for now.*

Dad, who has you? Have you figured that out yet? He was so relieved to hear Riordan's voice that he had to take several deep breaths even to answer him through their link. *It's going to be fine, Dad. Stormy and Nikki have a plan.*

Them girls are gonna get themselves hurt, is what they're going to do. Riordan laughed. *I know they're about the best for the job, but I can still worry me some. I've never had daughters before, and I can't remember how to act around them three at times. They're not bringing Andi in on this, are they? That girl needs to keep my grandbaby safe.*

Andi is feeding us. And so you know, she's making your favorite pie for when you come home. He asked which kind. *Does it matter, Dad? You think they're all your favorite.*

Which was true. They really were. He loved pie more than he did most main courses. And he also knew what his son was doing. Distracting him so that he could think. Which he was better at now. He told Riordan that he loved him.

I love you too, Dad. More than I can ever tell you. You and Mom? Well, you've been the best parents any of us could ask for. I never told you this, but our friends were jealous that we had you when we were growing up. Ordan told him he was better now. *Tell me what you hear or smell. I know you can smell a cake coming out of the oven a mile away. Use that skill now, Dad.*

I can't smell any other animal around, shifter or otherwise. I'm thinking that I'm in the basement of something. I can smell blood... not fresh, but it's got a lingering smell of death to it. Riordan asked him if he could see anyone. *Not yet. But I've not moved around too much. Don't want them to know that I'm awake just yet. I can't hear anyone talking either. Might be that they forgot about me.*

Hardly. How did they get you, do you remember that? Ordan moved his head a little, careful of his aching head. There wasn't anyone near him, but he was still careful. *Nikki said to tell you good job on not letting them know you're alert yet. She said to remind you that there might be cameras pointed at you.*

He didn't lift his head any more than he had to, but did see that there were cinderblock walls in front of him and to his right. Also, the chair he was sitting in was stained with blood. He wasn't sure if it was his or not, but he had a feeling that it wasn't. He let Riordan know.

The chair they've got me all tussled up to has blood on it. I'm thinking it's not mine, or if it is, I'm a sight more hurt than I thought. But how they got me? Well, I was coming out of the Bakery. Had my hands full, so I set the bag of bread that your mom sent me in to get on the roof of the car to dig out my keys. Someone said something behind me, like "you'll have to do" or something like that, and then I was flipped around to face him. I got a good look at the feller but didn't know him. Riordan asked him to describe the man. *Tall, sort of unkempt, like he'd been on a drink and hadn't had time to clean himself up. But he smelled like…he had on too much cologne. Or he'd been around someone that did…. Not cologne, but perfume. He smelled of a woman's perfume. Expensive stuff. I think it's something that your mom wore before. And he had blood on his shirt.*

Ordan thought about that blood. It didn't look like he'd cut himself shaving, but that he'd been splattered with it. There wasn't much, just a few drops, but Ordan had thought at the time that someone had been murdered and he didn't want to be number two. He told his son what he'd thought, knowing that every little detail was helpful in some way.

That's good to know. We've come across some people that he might have killed. Or been there when they were murdered. There are also a few people we can't account for. Dad, can you hear anything that might tell us where you are? Like maybe a car or something? He tried his best to do what Stormy asked him to do, but he was thinking about the shoe that he'd only just noticed. He told her about it. *What does the shoe look like?*

Loafer. Like them kind that men wear when they want to look like they're not caring what they have on, but you know that they've spent a lot on them. He moved his head just a little more and saw him, the dead man. *It's a person on the inside of that shoe, darling. I'd say whoever killed him was pretty upset. There's a neat hole in his head and several, looks like as many as four, in his chest, and one in where his dick might have been. I think.... Someone is coming.*

He had no idea why he'd whispered to her. There wasn't any way for these fools to have heard him. And they were fools if they thought they'd get by with taking him from his family. But as soon as the two of them came in, he began to have his doubts on whether or not he'd make it out unscathed. He knew one of the men as well as he did his own wife. It was Otis Adkins from Nikki's paperwork.

"He'll have to be woke up soon. My daughter is coming here and I don't want her to find out what I've been up to until I can talk to her about Robert." Ordan told Stormy what he was listening to. "You're sure that Savannah has been taken care of?"

"Yes. Robert might have been a little more helpful had he known that she was fucking the limo driver and the guy who cleans his family's pool, too." They both laughed, and Nikki told him that Savannah was Otis's wife, and Robert was the daughter, Dorothea's, future husband. "I don't think he realized what a slut she was."

"Well, she's all done screwing me. And so far as I'm concerned, she got just what she deserved." Ordan wondered what that might have been, but decided that he really wasn't keen on knowing that. "Get something to wake him up with. I need to get this shit with Nikki taken care of. And so you know, the limo service called; they want to know how much longer we're going to be using the cars."

Ordan told his family to check with Roman Towing and Limo Service. *Roman is the only person around that has one of them suckers, and he's more than likely got a name on them too. Or at least a phone number.* Ordan felt pretty good about having something they could use. *I'm thinking that his wife has turned up dead somewhere too. He didn't enlighten me as to where she might be, but I'm thinking she's with a limo driver at home, as well as the guy who cleans the pool at this Robert's house.*

Robert Trevino. His family was found this morning. All shot in the head and left where they lay. There wasn't any forced entry, so it looks like the person who did this was known to the family, the cops are saying. The wife's body hasn't turned up as yet, but I'm having all new construction sites looked into in their area. See if any of them have some newly poured concrete. He didn't want to think about someone putting his body in the foundation of a building. Ordan told her he'd seen something like that on the television once. Nikki laughed. *Yeah, bad guys aren't hard to figure out for the most part. They're not the brightest bulbs on the Christmas tree, as my grandda is fond of saying.*

When water, colder than it was outside, hit him in the face, Ordan looked up at the two men and realized in that moment that he was in deep shit. Instead of showing them that he was afraid, which he was, he asked them what this was about.

"What this is about is that you're going to get me Nikki Neal. And then, so you're on the same page as we are, the two of you are going to be fodder in the landfill not far from here." Ordan didn't say anything, but did look down at the dead man on the floor. "That is my…well, was my future son-in-law, Robert Trevino. He, sadly, didn't play well with me, and I had to end his miserable life."

"Parked his car in your garage, did he?" That got him a fist to the face, and Ordan felt his head snap back. He supposed it was all right for the two of them to kid around about such things, but not him.

"You'll keep your mouth shut or I'll fucking kill you now and go back after your wife." He felt his cat move along his skin, and Ordan had to work very hard to keep him in check. When Bri spoke to him, he felt his entire being calm.

If you let that man make you shift and you kill them, I will be very upset with you. He asked her why. *Because he's kidnapped you, and that will be enough for the police to go in and investigate his life. I'd rather they did the killing than you. I have a grandchild coming that I'd like to share with you, and I don't want to do that between steel bars. Right now all they have him on is something to do with tax evasion. You'd think someone that had all that money would have paid his taxes to keep himself in check. But I guess when you have a criminal mind, you can just do as you please and think that's all right.*

I love you, my heart. She told him she loved him as well. *Tell them that there is a landfill not far from where I am that they're going to put me and this other man in. And darned if I don't smell Danish. The cheesy cherry kind. I'm thinking I'm not all that far from the Bakery.*

Can you see any windows? He glanced around and told Storm that he could see one, but it was one of them little bitty ones that were over doors. *Transom window. That helps. It means it's a house, not a business.*

He thought about asking her why when Otis started going on about how this was going to work. Ordan was going to call home, let them know that he'd been taken, and tell them that Nikki and nobody else was to go where he told her to.

"Do you know Nikki at all? I mean, the type of person she

is?" He told him he'd had the displeasure of working with her for a time. "Yeah, I'm betting you did. But she's not one to tell to do something. I mean, unless it was something you didn't really want her to do; telling her to do it is a sure fire way to get her not to do it. Maybe you should just talk to her. Might go over better."

"Had I wanted to talk to her, I would have." Ordan told his family what he'd said to the man. "Christ. A woman would have talked my arm off, but she would have done what I wanted by now. Perhaps I should just kill you and go after one of the other women in that house."

"You go on and think that might be a better bet. I'm thinking that you might not have done much research on them if you believe that they'd be any easier to handle than that wife of yours might have been." He asked him what he meant. But before he could answer him, Nikki said they'd found him. Ordan smiled. This was going to be over soon and he'd have some pie.

We're on our way, Ordan. You just sit tight and don't let them piss you off too much. And if you're not hurt when we get there, I might let you have a little fun with the prick. He told Nikki that he just wanted some pie. *You'll have it. I think Andi said something about apple and cherry. And there will be homemade ice cream too.*

Ordan started to tell Otis that the cavalry was coming, but he was hit from behind. When his already aching head exploded in pain, he knew as surely as he was sitting there that there was going to be hell to pay.

~~~

"You can't be serious." Apparently Aedan was when he said he was going too. "No you are not. I can't be worried about you and getting your dad out if you're with me."

"I know how to use a gun." Stormy said nothing but did

smile at them. "Tell her, Storm. Tell Nikki that I can use a gun as well as either of you."

"I'm not getting in the middle of this, but I will say that between the two of you, I'd much rather have her at my back than you. No offense. But she's got training that you don't. Hell, she's got moves that you couldn't do on your best day."

Nikki smiled at Storm and thanked her. But Aedan was pissed off and she was getting there too. They were wasting time and their dad was waiting for his pie. When she stretched her neck for the third time, it was her grandda that came to stand beside them.

"Son, let me ask you four questions, and if you can answer any of them without saying no, then I think she should let you go too." She opened her mouth to tell him to butt out, but he just raised his hand and asked to be heard. "It's a fair assessment to whether or not he can do this. Aedan, if you fail, are you willing to concede that you can't do this as well as they can?"

"Yes. But I can tell you right now, I can do this. And even though it's my dad, I won't freeze up." Her grandda nodded and sat down, asking Aedan to do the same. When he laid the gun on the table that her grandda had been carrying since she was a child, she waited too.

"Can you take it?" When Aedan reached for it, her grandda had it at his head before he could touch it. "Okay, try again."

Three times he wasn't able to get to the gun before her grandda had it pointed at him. The second test was one she'd passed only recently. She'd had to do it only once in her career, and that had been too many times.

"I want you to pick up the gun. I won't try and take it from you, but take it and shoot your brother in the leg." Aedan looked at Riordan, then at Grandda again. "Sometimes you have to shoot someone to get to the bad guy."

"I'm not going to shoot anyone I love. And I can't believe that you'd ask me to do that." Grandda lifted up his pant leg and showed him the scar that she'd put there. "You're going to tell me that you shot yourself to get to the bad guy?"

"No. No, Nikki shot me. It was either make me too difficult for them to take, or they got away. Sometimes, like I said, the good guys have to be taken out of the picture. Can you shoot your brother without hesitation?" Aedan said that he might be able to. "Okay, I'll let you slide on that. For now, anyway. Third question. What does this mean?"

The hand signals were as much a part of her conversation when working as using her words. The index finger and thumb out meant weapon, which Aedan knew, but when Grandda lifted it above his head, Aedan guessed.

"Take the gun? I don't know that." Grandda told him it meant rifle. The next two, point of entry and hostage, he didn't know either. "What does this have to do with me going with her?"

"You want them to be killed? Because as surely as you ask the first question of them, either of them, the bad guys are going to know you're around." Aedan looked at her and she could see the fear there, along with anger. "You want her to come home with your daddy? If so, then you stay here with me. But I'm telling you right now, I'm more terrified of her getting hurt than you are. Every time I look at her, I hear her telling me that they were there and then the gunfire."

"She's my world." Grandda said that she was his as well. Then Aedan looked at Grandda. "What was the fourth question?"

"If she's killed, will you be able to finish the job?" Aedan slid the gun to her grandda and stood up. When he left the room, his mom went after him and Storm told Nikki it was time to go. She was out the door when Aedan touched her mind.

I love you. With all of my heart. Please come back to me, and be safe. She told him she would try her best. *And Storm too. Watch each other's back for us all.*

Again, she told him she'd do her best. She and Storm moved along the outer edge of the Bakery, and she felt her mouth water at the smells coming from the place. They had thought about evacuating it, but were afraid that it would alert Otis that they knew where they were. But when Storm knocked on the back door, the signal that the people inside had been made aware of, the customers as well as the staff came out and ran to the street over from them. Storm looked at her when they were gone.

You ready for this? She told her she was. *Yeah, me too. They fucked with the wrong family taking Dad. I'm telling you right now, there won't be a trial for this prick. I'm going to end his miserable life as soon as I get answers.*

If I don't beat you to it. As they made their way to the house where they were sure he was, Nikki thought of something else. *When this is done, I'd like to go into business with you. I'm to understand that you work for some pretty important people.*

Yeppers. Your uncle, I guess. Nikki smiled and said she'd never met him. *Well, as soon as this is over, we'll make plans to have dinner in the place. But I'm thinking that you'll be having a lot of dinners there when Aedan is president.*

You think he will be? Storm said that she was sure of it. *Do you think that it has occurred to Aedan that he'd been had?*

What do you mean? Nikki just looked at her, and when Storm got it, she laughed. *Christ, I didn't even get that. We don't need to use hand signals any more, not in this family. We'd just talk the way we are now. He's going to be pissed if he figures it out.*

Yeah, but he's safe for now, and that's all that matters.

They were near the building now, and Storm told her to go around to the side and meet her at the window that was open.

The houses on either side of the one that Ordan was in were empty. Not because they'd evacuated them, but because they were on the market. Nikki wondered why no one had renovated them yet, and Storm told her they weren't sold.

Pausing when Storm did, she heard them talking. It was Otis and Joe, his right hand man. And they were talking about Savannah, Otis's wife, in the past tense. Going to the door that would get them into the house, Nikki stopped Storm when she started to step on the stairs.

Old houses creak. Come around to the porch and walk along the foundation. It's a trick my grandda taught me, how to get in like Mickey. Took me a bit to figure out he meant just a mouse. Climbing up on the pretty wrap around porch, they were nearly to the door when it opened. Storm hit the man coming out with the butt of her weapon. And when he dropped to the floor, Nikki went to her right. Otis was coming up the stairs when she fired a shot at his feet and told him to stop moving.

"Nikki? What the fuck are you doing here?" She grinned at him. "Christ, will you never fucking do what is expected of you?"

"Nope. Come on now, we're going to go and check on my future father-in-law. And he'd better not be hurt, or so help me, there will be hell to pay." Storm followed them to the basement. When she started to drag Joe down with them, dragging him by his feet, Nikki pointed out that they might need him awake at some point. So the two of them carried him down the steps. "This was too easy."

"No shit." Picking up the half bucket of cold water that was near the door, Storm tossed it on Joe and he came sputtering awake immediately. Storm smiled at him. "Hello, dumb ass. How's it feel to know that you've been bested by the best?"

Having the two of them sit on the floor with their hands on their heads was done quickly. Nikki kept thinking that it had been entirely too easy to get in and get the two men. While she tried to think, Storm searched the two of them and tossed their weapons on the ground by the door.

"Do we call them and let them know that it's over?" Storm said she was used to dealing with the shoot now and ask about it later sort of way of doing things. "We're missing something. Something big. What is it?"

"Maybe we're just that good." Nikki asked her if she believed that. "No. You're right, this was too easy. And look at them. They know it too."

Otis was smiling and Joe looked like he was hurting, but wasn't saying much either. She started to ask them, knowing that she'd not get an answer, when she heard someone come into the building. Storm put her gun to Otis's head when he opened his mouth. Nikki stuck her gun in Joe's mouth when he did the same thing. Whoever it was, they knew him.

"Hello? Otis? Joe? Where are you?" Storm shook her head in answer to Nikki's silent question if she knew him. "Otis, I have that information that you asked for. Hello?"

As soon as the man entered the room, Nikki tossed him to the floor. When she had her booted foot on his back, she looked at Joe when he started cussing. Well, this was a nice turn of events, she thought.

"Unhand me, you fool. I'm the sheriff around here, and I won't have you treating me this way." She flipped him over and pointed her gun at him. "What the fuck are you? Ninjas?"

Both her and Storm were dressed head to toe in black spandex. She had never worn anything like this before, but found not only was it easier to move in than jeans and a tee shirt like she usually wore, but it made her feel sexy too.

"Yes, we're ninjas, and you're an idiot. What kind of information did you have for Otis?" When he didn't answer her, she kicked him in the ribs. She was sure that it wasn't painful; the man had to be carrying about fifty extra pounds of padding in the way of fat with him. "I asked you a question. What did you have for Otis?"

"I don't know who you're talking about." She just rolled her eyes at him. "Okay, I was playing them. When Joe there asked me to find some information on the Harrison family, namely Bri, I found it for him."

The gun going off in the small room made her jump. Joe was dead, his brains and blood splattered all over the wall behind him, as well as Otis and the sheriff. When she looked at the other woman, Storm only shrugged before speaking.

"They were going to take Bri. It's bad enough that they took Ordan, but to take that sweet woman just doesn't set right." Nikki had to hold back a smile as she continued. "I think my finger slipped. That's what I'm going to say if asked. It was an accident because I was so nervous."

Nikki didn't think anyone would ever believe that Storm wasn't in complete control all the time, but said nothing. Otis was screaming about murder, while the sheriff, Dave Wyler, was crying about how he'd only come in when he'd found the door opened. Ordan woke to that and smiled at her.

"Hello, my darlings. You come to take me home?" Storm laughed and so did Nikki. This family was certainly going to be fun to get to know, that was for sure.

CHAPTER 11

Aedan was biding his time. He knew that they had to be talked to…briefed, Riordan called it; questioned, Paddy called it. Either way, he had to wait until they were released before he could have his turn at his mate. And he wasn't sure if he was going to be pissed first or just glad to see she'd made it out alive. He'd been tricked. It had taken him nearly ten minutes after they left to figure it out.

"That alone should tell you that you were better off here." He asked Paddy why. "You figured it out, for which I'm glad…I'd hate to have my little baby married to a man who couldn't think on his feet, but it took you too long. Next time you'll be better, but this time, I think you might have gotten them hurt."

"Neither of them were even touched." Paddy said that he knew that, this time they'd been all right. Aedan wanted to be pissed, but Paddy was much too calm for him to be more than mildly annoyed. "How did you allow her to do this? I don't mean becoming a cop, but leaving the house every day knowing that you might not see her again. I don't know that I'll be able to do it."

"You hurt for them. If you tried to tell her to stop it, doing something that she loves so much, she'd do it for you. In a heartbeat. But she'd be unhappy and you know it." Aedan said he would as well. "See, that's what you have to do. Learn to say you love them every minute you have them with you. Because you know as well as I that either of you could just be crossing the street at any time and get yourself killed. Or that you could lose a child to some senseless act and have your life crumble when the other half of you hides in their head." Aedan knew he was talking about his own wife.

When they brought the body bag from the basement he wondered what had happened there, but didn't care so long as it wasn't his family. Adkins was brought out next, his arms cuffed behind his back, his body covered in blood. When he was put in the back of the cruiser, Mac came to stand next to Aedan and asked him if he was all right.

"I am. Is Andi okay?" He said she was baking, something she did when she was upset. "Good. You should be about as big as a house in no time if her being upset is all it takes. I love her, too. You know that."

"I do, and thank you. Ennis is looking Dad over. He was asked to by the Feds that showed up about an hour ago to make sure that he'd not been hurt. I heard one of them say that Dad was fine but going on about pie. Andi will be thrilled to know that he's told several men they could come and have a couple of slices with him."

Aedan nodded and tensed up when Ennis came out with their dad. "He's fine. Nothing but a headache that will be gone as soon as he shifts."

The rest of his brothers were there as well, and each of

them hugged their dad before Mom got to him. Aedan made his way to his dad and took the big hug in stride. Patting him on the back, they both held each other just a little longer than the others had. His dad was just fine. And so was Nikki.

The Feds were taking over. Aedan had heard it was because it was a multi-state issue, but Paddy had told him that it was more than that. It wasn't until the motorcade pulled up that he remembered that Paddy was Howard's dad. He had no idea who might have called him until Paddy went to him and was hugged. Then Howard came and stood next to him.

"Is she all right?" He told him that he'd not been able to see her yet, but Ennis said she was. "Good. This is going to end a great many things for her, my showing up. She's not going to be happy."

"You're going to out her." He nodded. "Why would you do that? I mean, she loves what she does."

"Because, my dear boy, I can't have my future replacement's wife working undercover when she needs to be picking out her presidential plate pattern." He looked at the house, then back at him. He could only imagine what she'd pick. "Besides, it's time, don't you think, that I acknowledge her for a job well done? She's been working very hard, and has been beaten up enough for several lifetimes."

Aedan didn't think she'd see it that way. And he was pretty sure she was going to hurt her uncle when she found out what he was up to. But as soon as she came out of the house with Storm, he made his way to her. All thoughts of undercover took on an entirely different meaning to him. He needed his mate.

As soon as he was close enough to touch her, she backed away. His heart shattered in his chest and he felt like he'd been slapped. But she smiled at him and he reached for her again. This time she held out her hand to stop him.

"They need to take my clothing." He growled. "For evidence. Joe was killed while we were down there, and they want to be certain that Storm and I are telling them the truth."

"You had to do it." She shook her head and he waited for her to say more. But when she looked over at Storm, then turned and smiled at him, he asked her what had happened.

"Her finger slipped." They both looked at Storm, then at each other again. He burst out laughing. It defused his anger and hurt just in that moment. Both of them were still laughing when she was led to a small room and given a pair of scrubs to pull on.

When she came out of the room, he picked her up and was headed for his car when he was stopped by men in suits. He wasn't going to play nicely if they tried to stop him again. The first man smiled and asked if the president could have a word with Nikki.

"No." The man cleared his throat. "You asked, I answered, I said no. Go away. She's my mate, and I can't be without her much longer."

"He said to remind you that you have a dinner engagement in twenty minutes." Aedan wanted to scream. "And he also said to tell you that things are set up for you nicely. That Browning helped."

"The only thing I want help with is getting away from here." The man nodded. "I swear to Christ, this is not making me happy."

"Yes, sir, I can see that, but the sooner you get this over with, the quicker you can take her back to your home and *talk*." He made the word talk sound like he no more believed that was what they were going to be doing than Aedan did. "In two hours tops, you're going to be done."

He wasn't going to be that lucky. When Nikki was led away for the second time, Aedan figured that the man was right. The sooner they were all satisfied that they had all their answers and the bad guys were gone, he'd be able to spend a long time with her in his arms. As soon as she realized where she was going, Nikki turned to look at him.

"You did this?" He said that he had nothing to do with it. "You do know that once this hits the papers, and there is no doubt that it will, I'm done as an undercover cop."

"That's what I told him. But he said that he wanted to talk to you and this was the only way." She nodded and looked at Howard, but didn't move. He leaned into her throat and nipped at her skin there, and then bit her earlobe. "I want you to do this so we can go and out the governor. After that, you're going to be naked and over my cock before we even get to the house."

"You promise?" He said that he did. "All right, but I'm telling you right now, I'm not going to be nice at dinner. I'm hungry and pissed off. This Ellison person is just one more cog in my wheel of shitty shit going on."

"I expect you to be no nicer to him than he's going to be to us." She turned and looked at him. "This meeting is not going to go as he plans. And I'm done fucking with him."

She looked back at her uncle before speaking. "When you're president, you'd better never make a person wait to get laid. Or me for that matter." He said he'd never do that. "And I want to work with Stormy if she'll have me. I think the two of us will do good things."

"She'd be lucky to have you. If she doesn't want to, you can open your own private practice, and you and your grandda can be private investigators if you want." Nikki said she liked that idea. "All right, let's go and talk to your uncle, then have a terrible dinner with Ellison. After that, naked and fucking shall commence."

When she got to the president, Nikki was smiling. He wasn't sure if it was because of what he said or that she was thinking of something evil to do to his body. Whatever she wanted, he was game. Aedan wasn't going to let her out of his sight again if he could help it.

He was also going to marry her, legally. As soon as it could be arranged. While the two of them spoke, Aedan reached for his mom. He knew that she'd be able to get a quick wedding together better than anyone.

You'll have to give me a couple of days to plan. I'm so happy to have your dad back with me. He told her he was as well. *I'm glad that you're marrying her, but I'm thinking that you might want to have something bigger. A large wedding with lots of guests.*

Why would we want that? It was okay for the others to have a little ceremony. She laughed. *Mom, what are you planning?*

The future president will need the votes, don't you think? And what better way to get those than a lavish beautiful wedding with lots of family and friends. He liked her thinking. *Of course you do, son. I'm your mother after all.*

~~~

Nikki hated the dress she had on. And it felt like she was too exposed. But every time she tugged at the front of it, Aedan would put it back to rights. She finally gave up and asked him what they were doing tonight.

"Ellison thinks that he's going to talk me into not running against him this term. I think. Anyway, he's sent in a crew of men, his men, to bug the entire restaurant and to plant a few of his men in the place to listen in. Howard told me that there were nine cameras in the place, and two recorders. I can't wait to see his face when we're shown to an entirely different room than the one he's had set up." Nikki asked him why that was going on. "Howard is going to join us for a drink before. I think that will make the man sit up and take notice of me, don't you?"

"You're hard not to notice." He smiled at her. "I don't understand why he'd think this was going to work with you. I mean, I've read your stand on things…your proposals when it comes to jobs and other issues that have come up. And I know you well enough to know that you'll get them done too, no broken promises from you."

"I like that. I might use that as a slogan. No broken promises, Harrison." She told him it sounded stupid. "No, it doesn't. It's perfect. But in answer to your question—thank you for trusting me, by the way—he hopes to make me look foolish in just the way that you told me he would. Or if need be, make me appear to be foolish. Hot tempered too, I think."

"You're the most level headed person I know. Except when it comes to me." Aedan told her that it was because he loved her. "And I love you as well. But seriously, this thing is going to backfire something huge. He has to take that into consideration. I mean, he's taking a huge chance with this."

"I don't know, to be honest. But whatever it is, we're going to come out on top, I think." She hoped so too. "I'm getting a late start on this election. I know that and so does Ellison. Whatever he has in his head, it's going to be huge and explosive."

"I've had enough shit going on today. Let's try and keep the exploding to a minimum if you don't mind." He laughed and she leaned back against the seat. "I'm exhausted. When this is done, I want a nap. For about a week."

She must have dozed off, because the next thing she knew Aedan was waking her up. Getting out of the limo, she stood in front of one of the prettiest buildings she'd ever seen. Then she remembered the houses that they'd seen when getting Ordan out, and decided to ask Aedan about them.

"Riordan owns a lot of empty buildings downtown. He and Storm are working to get more businesses to come to the area and fill the shops again. What is it you had in mind?" They were taken to the bar where Ellison was, and she looked up at Aedan to answer him. "You look at me like that too much and we'll never make it to the salad."

"Behave. I thought they'd be nice shops, yes, but I was thinking like something fun. My grandda has always wanted to have a fishing store. Mostly I think it was just a place he could play in. He makes flies for fly fishing. Sell some bait and a few other things that the rich think they need, but mostly a place he could work his hobby in." Aedan said he liked that idea. Then he asked about the other building. "A Christmas shop. Opened year round, and full of only things that are for the holiday."

"You love Christmas." She told him it was her favorite time of the year. "All right. As soon as we get up tomorrow or the next day, I'll look into it for you. It'll be a nice investment for us, and you can play there when you're not working with Storm."

Before she could tell him she wasn't going to turn it into a shop for herself, they were standing with Ellison. The man gave her the creeps, and when he put out his hand for her to shake, she felt her cat run over her skin. Apparently, she didn't care for him either.

"You were right about this place, Aedan. Very nice place. I don't get to go out as much as you young people do, but that's something that comes with the job of being governor, I guess." He laughed like he was making a huge joke. "We're going to be seated now that you're here. I hope you don't mind, but I went ahead and ordered us a few appetizers to start with."

"Not at all. I want to introduce you to my wife, Nikki Harrison." It was the first time someone had called her that, and she thought it sounded wonderful. "Nikki, this is Dewey Ellison and his wife…I'm sorry, I didn't catch your name."

"Its Dyana with a 'y.'" Nikki was still trying to figure that out when the woman rolled her eyes and said she had to use the ladies' room. "I thought for sure that we'd be eating by now. I've been with the hairdresser all day. Who does your hair, if you don't mind me asking?"

"My hair? I guess that would be me. When it gets too long or won't stay in one of those rubbery things, I hack it off until it's out of my face, but that's about all I do to it." It was a lie. Nikki had her hair done by a professional when it needed cutting. But the look on the other woman's face was just what she needed to keep her from being bored. "The last time I was at Wally World getting me some new clothes — by the way, don't you just love this dress? Anyway, they had a two-fer coupon. You know, buy a haircut, get one for free? But since I was alone, I didn't bother then. Maybe you and I can go back sometime and share the cost. I'm sure they can fix you up like you are now."

The woman was horrified. Whether it was at her suggestion that she go to get their hair cut at a department store or that they use a coupon, Nikki wasn't sure, but they were coming out of the bathroom together when she saw her uncle in the next room. Shit was about to get real.

Ellison was talking to Aedan. Or more like, at him. He was telling him all the bad things that came with being the governor. No time to do things. There weren't late night dinners with friends. And no long vacations when the job was too much. Aedan took her hand in his before he spoke to the governor.

"Really? I heard that just two weeks ago you and someone went on a long cruise and had a wonderful time. I think I might have even heard that you were having a little too much fun, if you know what I mean." Ellison did not look happy about that. "As for late night dinners, I know for a fact that you have had more parties at your home than the last several governors have had their entire terms combined."

He blustered. Ellison was clearly embarrassed and upset, but Aedan only smiled at him and waited. Sometimes, she told him, less really was more. When the waitress told them that their table was ready, Ellison moved in front of them, cutting them off when he thought he knew where they were headed. When the waitress stopped him, Ellison was confused.

"No, I was told that we'd be sitting over there. Near the fireplace. Where it was quiet." Aedan said nothing but she watched his face. Here was a man who knew the ropes. And he had Ellison right where he wanted him. "I'm sure that there has been some sort of mistake."

"Hello, darling." When Uncle Howard joined them, Ellison was dumbstruck. And when he kissed her on the cheek and then hugged Aedan, Dyana smiled like she'd been awarded Miss Universe. "Hello. You must be Dyana Ellison. I'm Howard Wayneright, President of the United States. And you must be Dewey Ellison. I've heard so many things about you."

"Yes, yes. I'm so glad you could...you two know each other?" Aedan said that they did and left it at that. "I mean, you seem to know each other really well. I thought...that ad, I thought for sure you'd paid him to do that for you."

"Oh no, I can't be bought, like some people." There was

a tone there, one that implied that they all knew that Ellison was taking bribes. Which he was. "I thought that since I was in town, I'd join my niece and her new husband and talk about things. I'm sure you don't mind me joining you, do you?"

"Oh no. Niece? Mrs. Harrison is your niece? That would make Aedan here your...." Ellison looked at her. "You're his niece?"

"I am. And yes, because of our marriage, Aedan is his nephew. Nice how that works out, don't you think?" He nodded, but she was sure he was still trying to process things. "Can he join us for dinner?"

Dyana nearly knocked her husband over getting herself close to Uncle Howard. "You can come and have dinner with us any time you want."

"But I had things set up out here." Aedan asked Ellison what he might have had to set up and he flushed. "Nothing. Nothing at all. Of course, sir, you can join us. I'm sure that we can make room at our table. Do you have a place for the five of us?"

"We've set up a room, sir. Private." Ellison nodded, but he obviously wasn't thrilled about having his plans thwarted, and by the president no less, Nikki noticed. But there was little to nothing he could do about it now. The host leading them to the room continued, and Nikki nearly burst out laughing when Ellison looked crestfallen. "We've done a sweep, sir, as you have asked. All devices have been taken out. Thank you for letting us know to check on that. It was quite shocking."

They weren't the only people in the large room. The men standing around the outside of the room were all wearing the same type of suit, and she'd bet anything that they were armed not just with the guns that she could see, but more. As soon as they were seated, food was brought to them, large platters of appetizers, and their drink orders were taken.

"So, you said you wanted to talk to me about the debate." Aedan was filling his plate with potato skins, so he missed the look on Ellison's face. It was pure terror. "I have been giving it a lot of thought, the reasons you gave me about me not wanting to be governor, and I think I can handle them."

"You gave him reasons for not wanting your job?" Uncle Howard winked at her as he asked Ellison the question. "What sort of reasons might that be? And so you know, I think that Aedan here would make a great governor. It's a good starting point in his career, don't you think?"

"We have a second debate the week after Thanksgiving, and he wanted to give me a heads up on some of the things that he's not taken care of in his term. You know, promises that he made to the people and hasn't followed through on as yet." Uncle Howard nodded and asked what Aedan would do about them. "Well, he made a promise for more jobs. I was wondering about that one most of all."

"I've one company in the works that I can't discuss just yet." Uncle Howard just stared at Ellison, as if to say "You're seriously not going to tell the leader of the free world?" "There are people involved in this that would like to remain anonymous for a little while longer."

"All right. But what sort of business? How many people are they planning to hire? Have you suggested tax breaks? And if so, for how long?" Aedan leaned back in his chair as he continued firing questions at the other man. "Will they be using people here to build, or do they have their own companies? I'm assuming that they'll be using our highways as well as some of the other things we have to offer. Is there something in their package for that as well? The unemployment rate in Ohio and the nation is at four point nine percent. In some counties here, it's almost as much as thirteen percent. We need more than just one company coming in here to help out, we need a lot of them."

"There is just the one company." Ellison pulled at his collar and then drank a glass of water before continuing. "It's still in the infant stages for the moment."

"Infant? You've served two terms. Eight years, and you've still only got to the baby part of getting jobs for the state?" Aedan shook his head as if he was shocked. But she knew for a fact that he knew who the company was, how many they were hiring, and the answers to all of his questions to Ellison. "I'm sorely disappointed, Ellison. I certainly am. I'm thinking that the people are going to be upset with you, running on the same ticket and no more than baby steps in fulfilling even one of your promises."

"And I suppose you could do better? Tell me, Aedan of the great Harrison family, what is it you'd do?" Ellison's face turned bright red in his anger. "I suppose you'd pay people whatever they wanted to come here, set up, and just go away after you were elected. That won't work."

"I would guess you figured that out as well, didn't you? How do you plan to replace the money that had been earmarked for education and roads? You did dip deeply in that fund, didn't you, Ellison? And for what? Nothing so far as I can see. The land that you promised those men is still sitting there, with nothing more to show for your thievery than scrub and trash." Ellison looked around; he knew he was caught. "What I would do, and have started the process regardless of my getting into the governor position, is hire a team to look for jobs. Not just here, but the entire state. You'd be surprised at how many people are willing to not just let our people build their plants, but work in them as well. It cost me very little when you think of all the money that it will bring here. Jobs are just the tip of the iceberg. There will be money for education and programs for the elderly. Bus lines in the lower income areas that will help workers get back and forth to work. In addition to the jobs, my research has shown that welfare costs will go down, small businesses and boot strappers starting new businesses will have a chance to grow and hire more. Businesses beget business, my dad always told me. And sometimes you have to spend a little of your own money to make more."

Ellison said nothing. Nikki wasn't sure what he could have said other than to congratulate Aedan on his thinking outside of the box and doing the job he'd been paid to do. Of course that wasn't going to happen, but it would have been nice.

"I think, Dewey, that you'd be better off just conceding that you've lost this race and back off now." Ellison looked at Uncle Howard when he spoke quietly. "You've lost this war, but you don't have to be made to look foolish any longer if you just back off."

"No. I won't. I'm going to win this." Ellison looked at Aedan. "You give me that list of names so I can use them. I'm the governor of this state, and it's my responsibility to get businesses here, not some upstart like you. Give it all to me and I won't follow through on my other plans about you and your family."

"I'm assuming you're talking about the tax lean you plan on putting against my sister's restaurant and bakery? Or do you mean my brother's practice being fined large sums of money for things that we can't find in any books anywhere? Why would a doctor who only has a small practice have to have a vault bigger than the local bank for drugs? Or do you mean trying to ruin me with recordings of this meeting? I think you missed that boat when I had someone come in and sweep for the devices that you put in here. Also, so you know, I'm pressing charges on that. Your men, they were very helpful in telling us not only who had given them the orders to illegally record a private meeting, but also showed me the paperwork with your signature on it." Ellison stood up, but before he could move, three of the men around the room moved as one and stopped him. "You're being detained, Ellison. For reasons I'm sure you don't need me to list."

"No. You can't do this to me. I have plans. A great many of them. You'll see. Give me the list and I'll look good, and then I'll cut you a deal on...on whatever you want. Just don't do this."

He was taken away, his hands in cuffs, and his wife, Dyana with a "y," was right behind him. She kept talking about the mansion and asking how was she going to be there without him. When the door closed behind them, Aedan let out a long breath and Nikki reached for his hand.

CHAPTER 12

Aedan wasn't sure what he was supposed to do now. Food was brought to them; he supposed that he ate it, but when his plate was taken away, he had no idea what he'd eaten or how much. Looking at Howard when he laughed, Aedan felt his face heat up.

"You did well. Are you back with me now?" He nodded and looked around for Nikki. "She went to the ladies' room. I asked her if I may have a private word or two with you."

"I think I just made a very powerful enemy in that man." Howard told him that he might have, but it mattered little. "Really? Because with the shit I found out, I'm pretty sure that he can ruin me and my family without any trouble."

"He's no longer governor." Aedan looked around, then back at the president. "You did that very well. The things that you brought up, some of them I'd not found as yet. I would have, but you did a wonderful job of not just outing him, but bringing to light a great many things."

"They were easy to find once I started looking. And

Storm helped me. She, as you know, knows someone who knows someone." Howard nodded and pulled out a cigar and chewed on the end. "Do you ever light that thing? I mean, every time I see you, you have one that you simply chew up and then toss out."

"At one time I smoked them regularly. But since there is no more smoking in public places, I stopped. I'd be a hypocrite if I felt that I was above such laws, don't you think?" Aedan nodded. "But back to Ellison. You played him well. And knowing that he'd bugged this place? That was brilliant. How did you know?"

"Nikki. She told me when I set this meeting up that he would use whatever he could to make me look bad. She's going to help with a few projects in the downtown area here." Howard nodded and smiled. "We're not married, as you know. My mom is working on it. She said that we need huge, not a wedding at home like we were planning."

"Yes, the world will need to know that you're really married, as well as family and friends there to make you look like a good family man. You're going to make a fine president, Aedan." He wasn't so sure and said as much. "I think so. You're brave...it took a lot of guts to do what you did tonight. Smart...looking into Ellison was something I would do, but I've been bitten by that kind of bug before and not come out so well. And you're willing to ask for help when you think you might need it. Stormy told me that you went to her almost as soon as you hung up the phone with Ellison."

"I'm not Superman like some people are." They both laughed. "Do you know what happens now? I mean, the seat is vacant."

"You take it over. Run the state like you want for the end of the term. Use that for your next term. I don't think you'll have any trouble. Then after that, you move up and into where I am." Aedan said nothing. He wasn't sure what to say or to even think. "I can't come to you again, you know that, don't you? Not to say I won't help you. But from a distance from now on."

"I appreciate everything that you've done for us so far. You have no idea how much." Howard nodded. "To be honest with you, when you first spoke to me about this, all I could think about was how much I wanted this. It never entered my mind what I might do once I got there. But then I started looking at the things that others before me had done and not done. By the way, that list is longer than the first one. They promised a great deal but came through on very little, if any of it."

"It's why I think you'll be good at this. The governorship is the perfect place for you to start too." The cigar was put on the ashtray that had been provided and he stood up. Nikki came in the room then, and Aedan stood as well, pulling her into his arms. "The two of you are going to be good for this state. I can't wait to see you in action when you get things going."

When he left them, Aedan sat down with Nikki in his lap and realized that two of the men were still there. When asked, they said that they'd been ordered to protect the new governor until things were settled. Aedan just needed a minute.

"You do know that once we're home, things will be quiet. For a little while anyway. Your mom needs me to help her with the big dinner." Aedan grinned. "Yeah, I explained to her the extent of my cooking abilities and she said I'd be fine. Just what is it I have to look forward to?"

"Washing dishes? Setting the table? I bet she makes sure you're a part of things." They stood and made their way to the front door. "What I'd really like to think about is taking you home and ravishing you for about two hours, then making love to you the rest of the night."

"I like that plan." On the ride home, he told her what Howard had said. "He told you before, when you were zoned out eating. I had no idea where you had gone, but you were really spaced out."

"I don't think I know what I was thinking either. Just blank." He looked out the window at the things around the town that he'd been here to see begin. The new restaurant that Stormy had going before he knew her was doing very well. More shops were opening downtown now, so there were simply more people moving around the sidewalks. Ennis's offices would be open in a few weeks and he'd be seeing more new patients. Darcy had purchased a large closed up hotel and was living in part of it while he renovated the rest. Liam was working hard at his projects, whatever they might be, while working at the family business too. Aedan wondered what else was in store for the Harrison ambush, and was looking forward to finding out.

~~~

Nikki wasn't afraid of being found…her white tiger coat against all the snow was helping her hide very well. Besides, if Aedan should find her, he'd just tell her to try harder at keeping hidden from him and they'd start again. She thought she had the perfect place this time…in the open and as still as she could be.

Did you know that every time you touch something, you leave your scent? It fades after a while, so unless you're smelling every twig you've brushed by it might be harder. She said nothing to him, knowing that he was trying to make her worry so he'd feel that too. *Also, when you just lay still, as you are right now, your scent gets stronger around you.*

It does not. He laughed and told her that it did. Standing up now, she saw him, sitting in the snow about five feet from her. *You're not helping me at all, did you know that?*

Yes. That took the wind out of her kite. *I want to be able to find you. However, if a human came upon you, in the snow, they'd never see you until it was too late.*

Have you ever killed anyone? When he didn't answer her right away, she moved to where he was. Rubbing her body over his, she could smell what he meant. His scent was stronger where he stood. *I love you very much.*

And I love you. My cat wants you. Then I'd very much love to take you as well. The purring sounds startled her; the cat, it seemed, liked that idea as well. *Run for us.*

She took off running as soon as he told her to. There was no point in hiding now; she was as needy as her cat and knew that he could smell it. She did, however, make sure that she touched the least amount of branches as she could, and tried not to brush up against any trees. When he caught her, tumbling her ass over head, she laid there thinking that there could be worse things in life.

His cat loved to dominate her. Nikki didn't mind so much so long as he made her come several times as a person. When he mounted her from behind, his big body pressing her smaller cat to the ground, the cat snarled at him and tried to knock him off. Of course, it never paid to be easy either.

His cat took hers hard. It was quick too, too fast for her to have enjoyed it, but that was fine. Nikki knew that he'd more than make up for it when he took her human part. Shifting when he told her to, she rolled to her back and watched the big cat move around her, as if he were trying to decide where to begin.

Christ, he wants you. She told him to get on with it then. *He's trying to decide if he wants me to have you first or him. I have no idea why it matters. We're both going to enjoy you as much as we can.* Nikki spread her legs, then slid her fingers into her pussy. Offering her fingers to the big beast, she laughed when he took her entire hand in his mouth. *You're teasing a monster, you know that, don't you?*

"I don't care. Eat me or fuck me as Aedan, but do something before I do it myself." To prove that she could, Nikki put her fingers at her clit and stroked herself. "I'm so wet. And needy. Did you know that when I touch myself this way, all I can think about is your thick tongue touching me?"

His cat moved her hand and licked her from gate to clit. When he was satisfied that she wasn't playing in his toy box, she let him have her. Christ, the things this cat could do with his tongue made her think there wasn't anything better in the world.

She came two times before he slid his tongue inside of her. Each time he touched that special part of her, the area that would make her scream for more, she'd bow up off the ground. The roughness of it, the thickness of it took her to heights that gave her body such pleasure. And when she felt hands on her instead of paws, she looked down at Aedan.

"One of these days I'm going to tie you to the bed and have all of you." She told him he did now. "Not like I want when you're unable to touch me. I'd eat you for hours on end, never stopping, not even when you beg."

"You do that well enough now." He sucked her clit into his mouth and she screamed. "More. Please, I want more."

He played with her for twenty minutes. Bringing her so close to the edge that she was sure that she was going to die from the pleasure of it. And then he'd back off, bringing her no less pleasure but never giving her just what she wanted. When he sat up, his cock in his hand, she watched him fist himself as he watched her.

"Show me what you need. Touch your pussy for me." She moved her fingers over her swollen lips and spread them wide for him. "You're so wet. I can see how dewy you are from here."

"You make me that way. If I come will you come all over me?" He said yes, his voice strained with his need. "Then you have to fuck me. I want you to take me hard and painfully."

His cum set off her own body. She screamed through the climax, feeling it come from her very toes. And when he fell atop her, his cock didn't slide into her but pounded into her, making her think he wanted to become a part of her. He brought her twice more before he leaned into her throat and bit her.

Nikki knew that he was strong, but the way he was taking her; she knew that he had no idea how strong he really was. And she loved every minute of it. When she came again, this time biting him in the shoulder as he filled her, Nikki once again fell in love with the man above her and knew that for as long as she lived, he would be the only man she loved.

"Are you all right?" She turned in his arms; they'd been spooned together like this for half an hour or more. "I didn't hurt you, did I? I'm really sorry. I don't know what came over me."

"You were fantastic. I don't think I'll be able to walk right for a week." He kissed her and she rolled to her back while he looked down at her. "You are the best thing that has ever happened to me, you know that, don't you?"

"Yes. Because I feel the same way about you. I can't.... When I first figured out what you were to me, I was such a fuck up. Christ, the things I said to you, it's a wonder that you wanted to even be in the same state as me, much less let me love you." She grinned. "I'm surprised every day that you didn't shoot me."

"Me too, now that you mention it. You were such a prick." He kissed her again, this time taking her breath away. "Aedan, what do we do now? I just wanted to live a normal life, but I'm thinking that's out the door. Not that I don't want you to be governor or the president—I know you'd do a good job at both—but our lives and those of any children we have are going to be open to everyone that wants to see them."

"I've been thinking about that too. I really don't know. Howard told me that it's difficult but not impossible to have a real life. And as you can tell by Ellison and his wife, it can be too much fun too." They both laughed. "We're not going to let this rule us. Yes, we'll be careful, but not to the point where we hurt those around us. We'll raise our children the way we think best, and not let the world interfere with us. As much as we can." She nodded.

"Speaking of Ellison, what do we do about the mansion? To be honest with you, I'd rather just stay here. I know that it's there for us to use, but I love this house." He said he did as well and asked her what she suggested. "Well, this might sound stupid, but why not open it up? Let people go in, charge them a little that would go to keeping the place up, and let them see what they're paying for."

"I like that idea. We'll have to have security tightened up. And we'll have to make sure that anyone that comes to the house knows that too." She asked him who that would be. "I have no idea, but that was one of the things on the list that Storm gave me for being in politics. She also said to make sure that we don't do anything stupid. I wasn't sure what she meant by that, but I promised her we'd try."

Getting up and getting dressed, she thought of the buildings downtown, the shops that she wanted to get open. Her grandda had already bought one of them using his pension, and she was sure that he was going to live above the shop after renovating it into a nice little apartment for himself.

The phone was ringing as soon as they entered the house. Winnie answered it, then handed the phone to Aedan. Nikki left him to it, hearing someone saying they were a reporter before she left the room. She was surprised to find Andi sitting on the couch waiting for her.

"I wasn't here long if you're worried about that. Winnie, who I love by the way, said it would be all right." She told the woman of course it was all right. "I have a favor to ask you. Not a big one, and if you say no, that'll be okay too. I'm looking for a potter."

"A potter?" Nikki sat down and Rose came in with a try of scones and tea for the two of them. When she left them, Nikki smiled at Andi, who looked nervous. "I don't bite, you know. And I'd love to help you find this person. Who is it?"

"I know that, but I'm not terribly good around people. It's not you. But this potter, his name is Rickson. I've been able to find out that he's a recluse and that he's been a potter for over sixty years. His work is very famous." Andi sat beside her and showed her pictures on her phone. "Mac collects his work. Anyway, I want to find him to see if I can get him to do something for Mac for Christmas. I know it's not even Thanksgiving, but it's in a few days and from my research, I'm understanding that it takes time to throw a piece then get it fired and glazed."

"Where have you looked so far?" Andi told her that all she could find out was that he lived in the Smokey Mountains area someplace, and that at one time he had a shop, but no more. "What was the name of his shop, and do you know his first name?"

"It was just Rickson on the shop name. Rickson Pottery. As for his first name, I'm having trouble with that too. The initial looks like a *D* sometimes, and at other times like it's a *B*, so I'm not really sure." Nikki couldn't tell either. "I've been looking on the Internet, and I've even called a few dealers, and the only thing they can tell me is to contact his publicist. And that person, whoever it is, said that she'd try. Try what, I have no idea, but that's all I can get out of her. And there isn't a phone number either, just an email address."

"I'll do my best for you. Grandda might know someone that can help, I'll ask him now." Nikki messaged her grandda and asked him. Smiling when she was done, she asked about the baby. "You look so beautiful, glowing even. I know that you're not very far along, but you must be getting excited."

"I am. And so is Mac. He keeps telling me to take it easy, but I feel so good all the time. And Mom is knitting the cutest things for it." Nikki tried to think what it would be like to carry a baby, and decided that it might be something she'd like to do someday, just not right away. "You and Aedan, you're going to be moving soon, I guess."

"No, we're going to stay here. The house is paid for by the state and all, so we have plans for it, but we want to stay here, in our own home." Andi looked relieved. "What would you do?"

"Just what you guys are doing. I love the house we have and all the land around it. And if we want to redo something, we can without asking for permission. I'm to understand that that is something that you'd have to deal with."

"I never thought of that, to be honest." Her phone buzzed

and she looked at the message from her grandda. "He said to tell you that it's both...there are two of them. He's not sure why there is, but he's got someone looking into it. There are no names yet, but the initials as you have guessed are both the *B* and the *D*. He also said to tell you that for the last nearly thirty years there has also been an *RW* with a line under it above the name." She could see that he was still typing and waited for him. When the message popped up, she laughed. "He said that he's going to expect a payment from you in the form of a pineapple pie when he gets this for you."

"Deal." Andi laughed and stood up. "Tell Paddy that it's a secret, if you don't mind. And that if he would talk to you and not me about it, I think we can work this out. Thanks for your help on this, Nikki. I'm glad that you're a part of this family too."

After Andi left her, she checked on Aedan and Rose told her he'd gone to his office. Nikki had taken one of the rooms on this floor as her own and went there now. Time to have a little fun with this potter. Plus, she wanted to get her own Christmas list started and try to figure out what to get for her husband, five brothers, two sisters-in-law, as well as in-laws and her grandda. Not to mention staff. Her mind was still working around that when Grandda messaged her again. It was a link.

Daniel Rickson, 84, died peacefully in his sleep, it began. She read the entire thing, making notes on all the family names. There were four with the first initial *B*. Benson, Blake, Brody, and initials again, BG. There wasn't any mention of how they were related to the elderly man, only that they were family. She called Andi to let her know.

"Oh well, perhaps I can figure out something else." Nikki told her not to give up, her grandda had said there were two potters. "You think you can figure that out? I'm thinking this is why the woman didn't get back to me with much. He was more than likely ill."

"I would say that's a good bet. Let me do some more digging, and when I find out something, I'll let you know. Maybe they'll have a sale or something that we can go and find some of his pieces. Might be kind of fun. A road trip for the two of us." Andi laughed and said she was game.

Nikki worked for another two hours and found out that there was very little on Mr. Rickson and the BG person, but a lot on some of the other members of his family. It seemed that they weren't a nice friendly family either.

Benson had been arrested twice for grand theft, stealing a car once and robbing a gas station the second time. He was currently out on parole. Blake Rickson was semi famous as an artist, but had run into hard times for a while and didn't paint much anymore. There was very little on Brody other than to say that he wasn't very social nor did he like to have his picture taken. There were several shots of him with his hand up in front of the lens. She thought she also figured out the RW on the newer pottery. It was the name of the new studio, she thought. But the best news she'd found was that there was going to be an exhibit and sale of some of the Rickson pieces in Columbus in a week, and she'd been able to snag two tickets by calling in a couple of favors.

Nikki was enjoying herself, she realized as she made her way up to bed. Aedan had gotten called out on a business emergency, and she had been so busy that she'd opted to stay home. She might just talk to her grandda about becoming private dicks, as was suggested.

CHAPTER 13

Brooke sat near her great grandda's grave and looked around the beautiful setting where he'd been put to rest at. He would have absolutely hated it. Grinning, she described the area to him.

"You're under a great maple tree. I'm sure that when you picked this plot for you all those years ago you had no idea how much you'd come to hate maples. Anyway, you're right under it. I can almost hear you now; 'The damned roots will make my back hurt more.'" She giggled. "There is a little vase of flowers here. I'm not sure who would have brought them, but they're in an ugly plastic vase that looks like it might have been used before. I'm thinking that Mrs. Sheppard brought them to you. She never did like you."

Great grandfather had been gone for two weeks now, and she missed him more and more every day. Thanksgiving had been a bust, with her all alone having a pizza while crying her eyes out. He'd been her entire world, and now, like a tablecloth being ripped off a table with the stuff still on it, that was how she felt. The place settings all wobbly, but nothing to make it prettied up.

"Benson came by the house yesterday. He's pretty pissed off that you left it all to me. Thank you for that, by the way. I love that you gave me something to remember you by. Not that I need it, but I'm glad for the house and studio too." She looked at the family just down from where she was, and saw that they were going to have a picnic. Right on the grave next to them. "Brody has been staying with me, but I don't think that'll be for much longer. You know how he can get."

Benson, her brother, was a dick and a bastard. He was older than her by seven years, and lorded that over her whenever she didn't do what he wanted. Which was seldom since she'd grown up and gotten smarter. He was forever in trouble, and when he wasn't, he was about to be. Avoiding him had become nearly a full time job for her.

Brody was her baby brother by nearly two years. While he was loving and kind, he had his own set of problems. He had been diagnosed with social anxiety, or SAD, when he was about ten. He hated to be where people might judge him or look for things he might do wrong. There wasn't any real foundation for his fears, but he had them all the same. It didn't help him that her Uncle Blake and Benson would treat him badly when they were around him.

"I've heard from Mary again. She's going to have to go, I think. From some of the emails that she's sent me, it looks like she's being rude to people who contact her about you. I'll have another talk with her, but I don't think it'll do any good." She thought about the lovely condolence email that had been forwarded to her account that she shared with her great grandda. "I'm going to take that part of your life over when she's gone."

Brooke looked at her watch and decided that she needed to get back to the studio soon. There were things there that needed her attention. She blew a kiss to her great grandda and made her way to her car. Brody was there waiting for her. He had his bags near him, packed already.

"I'm going to go." She nodded and asked him if he wanted a ride. "Yes. To the bus station in town, please."

"There is no bus station in town, Brody. Can I take you to the airport?" He nodded but didn't look at her. She waited until he did. "Where are you going? Do you have money?"

"I don't know. The first place I see that looks good. And I have money. About two grand now." She nodded, knowing that he had plenty should he want it. Brooke took care of his accounts for him and made sure that he had good solid investments. "Benson is mad."

"Benson is always mad. What is he mad about this time?" Brody got into the car when she did. Waiting for him to buckle up, she knew better than to help him. He'd remember, but until then, she'd not move the car. When he was ready, she started for the airport.

"He's upset because you won't give him the house. I don't think you should either. He'd just sell it off then wonder where the money went. He asked me for some too. But I told him I was broke until next month." He grinned at her. "Uncle Blake is mad too. But not just about the house. He's mad because you got all of his things. You deserve them, Brooke. You took care of Granddaddy when he had that stroke. It should be yours."

"Thanks, Brody. He hated being so ill after leading such an active life. I miss him." Brody said he did as well. "Will you let me know when you get to where you're going? Send me a postcard or something. I'd like to hear from you."

"You going to that show? The one that Grandda put you

in?" She said that she didn't know yet. "I hope you do. Maybe I'll come and see you there. Nobody has to know who you are. Just like with Grandda."

Recluse. Hermit. Anchorite. Troglodyte. He was no more a caveman than she was a beauty queen. These were all names that her grandda had been called all his life. He told her once that it made him more famous, the fact that no one knew who he was. And when she began working in the clay with him, he'd told her to never let anyone know her first name. It would haunt her for the rest of her life. So she'd learned to mimic his signature but made hers a B instead of a D, as his name was. It had served her well too.

"I might go, then, if I have a chance to see you there." She knew that she had to go. She'd made a promise to him the morning he passed away. "I have all the pieces crated up. They're going to pick them up next week, after the first of the month."

"I saw them when I thought you were in there." She spent a great deal of time in the studio, and when she wasn't in there, she was in the firing room, where she and Grandda had built their kilns, both open air and closed. "You be safe, Brooke. You're all I have now."

"I promise, Brody. Do you want me to park and go in with you?" He said no, he'd be better on his own. "You call me, all right? I need to know that you're safe too."

"I will. As soon as I get it figured out." He got out of the car and she waited for him to close the door, but he got back in and kissed her on the cheek. She was so surprised by it that he was gone before she could do anything. Brooke cried all the way home.

There were two cars in her drive when she got there. One of them was her uncle's, the other she thought was her brother's. But the last time she'd seen it, it had been new; this one had been wrecked. A lot, it seemed. Both of them were sitting on the front porch when she got out, and stayed where they were when she joined them. There wasn't any way that they could get in without her and the keys. Not unless they wanted to be arrested again.

"I thought now that the old man is gone, you'd take the security off for us." She asked Benson why she'd do that. "Come on, Brooke. This is too much house for one person. I thought you'd let me stay here for a little while. You let Brody when he's around. Where is he, anyway? I think he was going to lend me some cash."

"He's left, and no he wasn't. You know as well as I do that he told you no. The same as I'm telling you about living here with me. No. I don't want you stealing from me again."

She sat down and waited for her Uncle Blake to speak. When he stood up, towering over her, trying to intimidate her, she pulled out her gun. He backed off with his hands in the air.

"You never were very nice to me." She told him because she didn't like him. "Now there you go, being all uppity to me. Don't you know that I'm your uncle? And that you should just bow before me?"

"Not going to happen. And I'd very much like it if the two of you got off my porch. I'm not going to invite you in, and I'm certainly not going to give you anything. You heard what the will said. You've both spent any good will that he had for either of you." Uncle Blake spit on the porch and she said nothing.

"I'm thinking you might owe us just a little more, don't you think, sister dear? I mean, you got it all. That ain't the least bit fair, now is it?" Brooke pretended to consider it, and told Benson she thought it was. "Why don't you just give us a couple of his pieces to sell off? I heard there was a bigger market for them now that he is dead. What are you going to do with them anyway? Look at them? Christ, woman, it's not like you don't have like a million pieces stashed in there. Just two each for us."

"Nope." She pulled her phone out and looked at the time. "You have two minutes to get out of here before I call the cops. I have a restraining order against you, Uncle Blake, and if you fuck with me, it'll land your ass back in jail. This time you'll be staying, too. You too, Benson. It's time you both left."

When he took a step toward her, she heard the low growl behind her. She knew it was the wolf that hung around the land, even knew that he was the local banker when he wasn't roaming the woods. Morgan Boyer had been a friend of her grandda's and hers for a very long time.

"You calling the dogs on me now? Brooke, you are... Christ." She turned when Uncle Blake backed away far enough to hit the wall behind him.

There were perhaps fifty wolves there, all of them large and dark. Their fur stood on end and their fangs were showing while they moved closer to the porch where they were standing. Morgan touched her mind and was laughing when he spoke to her.

He smells of fear. What I wouldn't give to see him wet his pants again. Brooke told him to behave. *I shall, Running Water. I shall.*

Morgan was part of the local tribe that lived in Cheyanne. There were others there, most of them simply human, but Morgan and his pack weren't people to fuck with. She'd seen him in action before. Brooke turned to her family.

"If you leave right now, I'll not tell him to attack. You know that I can, I've done it before." Benson nearly fell twice getting to his car, but Uncle Blake stood his ground. "You're not getting anything from me. Not a thing."

"There will come a time, Brooke, when you don't have these dogs here to protect you. And when you get there, I'm going to teach you a lesson that I should have years ago."

Brooke lifted her chin, showing him that she wasn't afraid of him anymore, when the truth was, she was terrified of him and her brother. As he moved by her, he reached out. When his fingers brushed her arm, she saw the black streak hit him in the chest. Morgan had her uncle down on the ground with his mouth around his throat.

Go in the house, Running Water. I will not harm him, but he won't leave here without giving me a taste of his blood. I promise you, it won't be nearly enough to kill him, as he deserves. Nodding, she did as she was told. Two of the pack entered with her, and she fell rather than sat on the couch. Neither of them came to her, but just knowing that they were there helped.

Brooke had no idea what she was going to do now. Her family wasn't going to let her live her quiet life any longer, she'd bet. When Morgan came in a few minutes later, Brooke burst into tears. It was suddenly too much for her.

~~~

Mac checked on his tickets twice as he made his way to Columbus. To think he was going to get to see his favorite artist. Or at least his work. He glanced over at his brother, Darcy, and asked him if he was as excited as he was.

"No one is as excited as you are. You're like a five-year-old at Disney. Christ, I can't believe I agreed to come with you." Darcy was joking and Mac knew it. He liked the guy's work too. Just not nearly as much. "We're going to have a lot of time between the show tomorrow and when we arrive. What do you want to do first? Mom wants us to pick up a few

191

things while we're at the North Market, and then Dad wants us to find a cigar shop to get something for Howard."

"I'm supposed to look for a place that sells antiques to see if I can find an old chest for the baby's room. Mom is getting it for Andi for Christmas. Also, we're to keep an eye out for anything that has to do with fishing. I guess Paddy loves old lures too." Mac had never had so many to buy for at Christmas. And he was loving every minute of it.

There were the aunts that had been adopted by the family, and Nikki's grandda that had filled that spot for them. He was glad now that they'd brought a truck with them. He was sure they were going to fill it before they left.

"I have a few places that I want to see about as well. I'm in the market for something to put in the second building I bought, and I haven't any idea yet what to put in there." Darcy looked a little frazzled, and Mac asked him what was going on. "I'm thinking of leaving the firm. I don't have a lot of interaction with anyone there anymore, and to be honest, I'm sort of burnt out in helping people get their businesses up and going. I want to do that for something I own."

"You mean go into business for yourself?" Darcy said yes, that was what he was thinking. "Good for you."

Darcy laughed. "I thought you'd tell me how much you needed me. How leaving the family business is a poor move. At least you could have given a little token sadness for me leaving." Mac felt his face heat up. "I'm kidding, Mac. Thank you."

"I just want you to do what you want. The rest of us are." Darcy nodded. "I've seen you talking to Dad about your building and how much fun you're having in renovating it. I know that you have help, but Dad said you were doing pretty much all of it on your own."

"I didn't have a clue how to hang drywall or to set a screw. I just thought, you know, that it just appeared." They both laughed. "Not really, but you know what I mean. Anyway, I think I'd be good at being a business owner. I've certainly got enough experience from others in how to make one fail."

They talked about it all the way to Columbus, only pausing long enough to get some dinner and gas. This was going to be fun. Not just because he was getting to do something that he'd wanted to do for a long time, go to an art opening, but he was going to get to do it with his brother. When they got to their hotel, he spoke to Andi.

How are you feeling? I really wish you could have come with me. She laughed and told him she was the same as when he left her just over two hours ago. *I know, but I miss you.*

This is good for you and for me. I'm getting to go shopping with Mom and the others in New York. I've never been there before. I've never been anywhere before meeting you. We're going to have a blast. He knew that too, but still missed being with her. *I got a card from Jim today. He sends his love. I'm going to go and see him when we get back. He wants to come here for the holidays.*

Great. I miss him as well. Tell him I got him something cool for Christmas. He'd found some model cars for him. The cars were from the fifties, an era that Jim loved, and they were going to put them together while he was there. *I'm hoping that when I get back, you and I can go on a run together.*

I'd like that as well. I love you.

After talking to her for a bit more, he could tell she was tired and they closed the connection. Mac was going to have a good time, try not to think too much about how he missed his wife, and hang out with his brother. He figured that two out of the three wasn't so bad.

He looked over at the piece that he'd gotten some time

193

ago, a Rickson crock that he absolutely loved. Nikki had told him that there was going to be a Rickson expert at the showing, and that she could tell him something about the piece. He was looking forward to knowing anything he could about the man and the crock. This was going to be the best time he'd had in a very long time, and he was glad that Darcy was here with him.

Harrison Ambush

Now Available

Coming Soon

Before You Go...

HELP AN AUTHOR

write a review

THANK YOU!

Share your voice and help guide other readers to these wonderful books. Even if it's only a line or two your reviews help readers discover the author's books so they can continue creating stories that you'll love. Login to your favorite retailer and leave a review. Thank you.

AWARD WINNING, BESTSELLING AUTHOR

Kathi Barton, author of the bestselling series Force of Nature, lives in Nashport, Ohio with her husband, Paul. In addition to writing full time Kathi likes to spend time with her eight grandkids, three children and three children-in-laws. She writes to relax and have fun.

Her muse, a cross between Jimmy Stewart and Hugh Jackman, brings them to life for her readers in a way that has them coming back time and again for more. Her favorite genre is paranormal romance with a great deal of spice. You can visit Kathi online and drop her an email if you'd like. She loves hearing from her fans. aaronskiss@gmail.com.

www.ingramcontent.com/pod-product-compliance
Lightning Source LLC
Chambersburg PA
CBHW032133170626
46808CB00006B/2218